Acclaim for Alice Walker and

POSSESSING THE SECRET OF JOY

"Walker celebrates joy and wholeness and has a sensual reverence for life; she is one of our most positive writers. . . ."

—*New Woman*

"A writer of staggering talent. . . ."

—New York *Newsday*

"A novel poised in its avoidance of polemics, confident in the grit of its language, and beautiful in its dual understanding of inhumanity and humanity . . . a staggering, but befitting, climax."

—*Booklist*

"Alice Walker can tell a tale. . . ."

—*Glamour*

"One of the most gifted writers of this country. . . ."

—Isabel Allende

"POSSESSING THE SECRET OF JOY offers a loud and clear voice crying out against a heinous practice that has been too long hidden behind millions of silences."

—*Chicago Tribune*

"[Alice Walker is] one of the best American writers. . . ."

—*Washington Post*

Meridian

The Color Purple

Books by Alice Walker

Revolutionary Petunias & Other Poems
In Love & Trouble: Stories of Black Women
Once (Poems)
Meridian*
The Third Life of Grange Copeland*
Good Night, Willie Lee, I'll See You in the Morning
You Can't Keep a Good Woman Down: Stories
In Search of Our Mothers' Gardens: Womanist Prose
The Color Purple*
Horses Make a Landscape Look More Beautiful
Living by the Word
The Temple of My Familiar*
Her Blue Body Everything We Know
Possessing the Secret of Joy*
Warrior Marks
The Same River Twice*

*Published by POCKET BOOKS

ALICE WALKER

POSSESSING THE
SECRET OF JOY

WASHINGTON SQUARE PRESS
PUBLISHED BY POCKET BOOKS

New York   London   Toronto   Sydney   Tokyo   Singapore

A Washington Square Press Publication of
POCKET BOOKS, a division of Simon & Schuster Inc.
1230 Avenue of the Americas, New York, NY 10020

Copyright © 1992 by Alice Walker

Published by arrangement with the author

Walker, Alice, 1944–
   Possessing the secret of joy / Alice Walker.
     p. cm.
  ISBN 0-671-78945-7
  1. Afro-American women—Psychology—Fiction. 2. Women immigrants—United States—Fiction. 3. Female circumcision—Africa—Fiction. 4. Abused women—Africa—Fiction.
5. Psychological fiction. lcsh.
  I. Title.
PS3573.A425P67 1997
813'.54—DC20

96-42270
CIP

First Washington Square Press trade paperback printing January 1997

10 9 8 7 6 5 4 3 2 1

WASHINGTON SQUARE PRESS and colophon are registered trademarks of Simon & Schuster Inc.

Cover design by Brigid Pearson
Cover photo by John Morrison/Photonica

Printed in the U.S.A.

This Book is Dedicated
With Tenderness and Respect
To the Blameless
Vulva

There are those who believe Black people possess the secret of joy and that it is this that will sustain them through any spiritual or moral or physical devastation.

*T*he children stood up with us in a simple church ceremony in London. And it was that night, after the wedding dinner, when we were all getting ready for bed, that Olivia told me what has been troubling her brother. He is missing Tashi.

But he's also very angry with her, she said, because when we left, she was planning to scar her face.

I didn't know about this. One of the things we thought we'd helped stop was the scarring or cutting of tribal marks on the faces of young women.

It is a way the Olinka can show they still have their own ways, said Olivia, even though the white man has taken everything else. Tashi didn't want to do it, but to make her people feel better, she's resigned. She's going to have the female initiation ceremony too, she said.

Oh, no, I said. That's so dangerous. Suppose she becomes infected?

I know, said Olivia. I told her nobody in America or Europe cuts off pieces of themselves. And anyway, she should have had it when she was eleven, if she was going to have it. She's too old for it now.

Well, some men are circumcised, but that's just the removal of a bit of skin.

Tashi was happy that the initiation ceremony isn't done in Europe or America, said Olivia. That makes it even more valuable to her.

I see, I said.

The Color Purple, *1982*

When the axe came into the forest, the trees said the handle is one of us.

Bumper sticker

PART
ONE

Tashi

I did not realize for a long time that I was dead.

And that reminds me of a story: There was once a beautiful young panther who had a co-wife and a husband. Her name was Lara and she was unhappy because her husband and her co-wife were really in love; being nice to her was merely a duty panther society imposed on them. They had not even wanted to take her into their marriage as co-wife, since they were already perfectly happy. But she was an "extra" female in the group and that would not do. Her husband sometimes sniffed her breath and other emanations. He even, sometimes, made love to her. But whenever this happened, the co-wife, whose name was Lala, became upset. She and the husband, Baba, would argue, then fight, snarling and biting and whipping at each other's eyes with their tails. Pretty soon they'd become sick of this and would lie clutched in each other's paws, weeping.

I am *supposed* to make love to her, Baba would say to Lala, his heartchosen mate. She is my wife just as

3

you are. I did not plan things this way. This is the arrangement that came down to me.

I know it, dearest, said Lala, through her tears. And this pain that I feel is what has come down to me. Surely it can't be right?

These two sat on a rock in the forest and were miserable enough. But Lara, the unwanted, pregnant by now and ill, was devastated. Everyone knew she was unloved, and no other female panther wanted to share her own husband with her. Days went by when the only voice she heard was her inner one.

Soon, she began to listen to it.

Lara, it said, sit here, where the sun may kiss you. And she did.

Lara, it said, lie here, where the moon can make love to you all night long. And she did.

Lara, it said, one bright morning when she knew herself to have been well kissed and well loved: sit here on this stone and look at your beautiful self in the still waters of this stream.

Calmed by the guidance offered by her inner voice, Lara sat down on the stone and leaned over the water. She took in her smooth, aubergine little snout, her delicate, pointed ears, her sleek, gleaming black fur. She *was* beautiful! And she was well kissed by the sun and well made love to by the moon.

For one whole day, Lara was content. When her co-wife asked her fearfully why she was smiling, Lara only opened her mouth wider, in a grin. The poor co-wife ran trembling off and found their husband, Baba, and dragged him back to look at Lara.

When Baba saw the smiling, well kissed, well made love to Lara, of course he could hardly wait to get his paws on her! He could tell she was in love with someone else, and this aroused all his passion.

While Lala wept, Baba possessed Lara, who was looking over his shoulder at the moon.

Each day it seemed to Lara that the Lara in the stream was the only Lara worth having—so beautiful, so well kissed, and so well made love to. And her inner voice assured her this was true.

So, one hot day when she could not tolerate the shrieks and groans of Baba and Lala as they tried to tear each other's ears off because of her, Lara, who by now was quite indifferent to them both, leaned over and kissed her own serene reflection in the water, and held the kiss all the way to the bottom of the stream.

Olivia

This is the way Tashi expressed herself.

The way she talked and evaded the issue, even as a child. Her mother, Catherine, whose tribal name was Nafa, used to send her to the village shop for matches, which were a penny each. Tashi would be given three pennies. She would lose at least one of them. The story she would tell about the lost penny might go like this: That a giant bird, noticing the shimmer of the coin in the glass of water in which she'd temporarily stored the pennies for safekeeping and for aesthetic enjoyment, had swooped down from the sky, flapped its wings so boldly that the glass of water fell from her hand, and when next she looked, having hidden her face from the creature for fear of its large beak and outspread wings, why— dash! No more penny!

Her mother would scold, or she'd put her hands on her hips, shake her head sadly and make a self-pitying cry to the neighbors about this incorrigible little liar, her daughter.

6

We were about the same age, Tashi and I, six or seven. I remember, as if it were yesterday, my first glimpse of her. She was weeping, and the tears made a track through the dust on her face. For the villagers, in gathering to meet us, the new missionaries, had raised a cloud of it, reddish and sticky in the humidity. Tashi was standing behind Catherine, her mother, a small, swaybacked woman with an obdurate expression on her dark, lined face, and at first there was only Tashi's hand—a small dark hand and arm, like that of a monkey, reaching around her mother's lower body and clutching at her long, hibiscus-colored skirts. Then, as we drew nearer, my father and mother and Adam and myself, more of her became visible as she peeked around her mother's body to stare at us.

We must have been quite a sight. We had been weeks on the march that brought us to Tashi's village and were ourselves covered with the dust and bruises of the journey. I remember looking up at my father and thinking what a miracle it was that we'd somehow—through jungle, grassland, across rivers and whole countries of animals—arrived in the village of the Olinka that he'd spoken so much about.

I saw that he too took note of Tashi. He was sensitive to children, and often stated as fact that there could be no happy community in which there was one unhappy child. Not one! he used to say, slapping his knee for emphasis. One crying child is the rotten apple in the barrel of the tribe! It would have been difficult to ignore Tashi. Because though many of the faces that greeted us seemed sad, she

7

was the only person weeping. Yet she uttered not a sound. The whole of her little cropped head and reddened brown face bulged with the effort to control her emotions, and except for the tears, which were so plentiful they cascaded down her cheeks, she was successful. It was a remarkable performance.

In the course of our daylong welcome, Tashi and her mother disappeared. Even so, my father inquired after them. Why was the little girl crying? he asked, in his stiff, newly learned Olinka. The elders seemed not to understand him. They shifted their robes, looked genially at him and at us and at each other and replied, looking about now over the heads of those assembled, What little girl, Pastor? There is no little crying girl here.

And Tashi and her mother did seem gone forever. We didn't see them for a long time, after they'd spent several weeks on Catherine's farm, a day's walk from the village. They turned up at vespers one evening, both Tashi and her mother dressed in new pink gingham Mother Hubbards with high collars and large flowered pockets, their faces similarly set in the look of perplexed, instinctive wariness that characterized Catherine's face whenever she encountered "the Pastor," as they all called my father, or "Mama Pastor," as they called my mother.

We did not know that on the morning we arrived in the village one of Tashi's sisters had died. Her name was Dura, and she had bled to death. That was all Tashi had been told; all she knew. So that if, while we were playing, she pricked her finger on a thorn or scraped her knee and glimpsed the sight of her own blood, she fell into a panic, until, gradually, she played in such a way as to take no risks and even learned to sew in an exaggeratedly careful way, using two thimbles.

But she forgot why the sight of her own blood terrified her. And this became one of the things the other children teased her about. And about which she would cry.

Years later, in the United States, she would begin to remember some of the things she'd told me over the years of our growing up. That Dura had been her favorite sister. That she had been headstrong and boisterous and liked honey in her porridge so much she'd sometimes stolen a portion of Tashi's share. That she had been very excited during the period leading up to her death. Suddenly she had become the center of everyone's attention; every day there were gifts. Decorative items mainly: beads, bracelets, a bundle of dried henna for reddening hair and palms, but the odd pencil and tablet as well. Bright remnants of cloth for a headscarf and dress. The promise of shoes!

Tashi

There was a scar at the corner of her mouth. Oh, very small and faint, like a shadow. Shaped like a miniature plantain, or like the moon when it is new. A sickle shape with the points toward her ear; when she smiled, the little shadow seemed to slide back into her cheek, above her teeth, which were very white. While she was crawling, she'd picked up a burning twig that protruded from the fire and attempted to put it into her mouth.

This was long before I was born, but I knew about it from the story that was often told: how bewildered Dura had looked, as the twig stuck to her lip, and how she, instead of knocking it away, cried piteously, her arms outstretched, looking about for help. No, they laughed, telling this story, not simply for help, for deliverance.

Did anyone help her?

This white witch doctor scribbles, only a little, behind his desk, on which there are small stone and clay figures of African gods and goddesses from

10

Ancient Egypt. I noticed them before lying down on his couch, which is covered by a tribal rug.

I think and think, but I can not think of the rest of the story. The sound of the laughter stops me before I can come to the part about the rescue of my sister Dura. I know that the twig, ashen, finally dropped away, having burned through the skin. But did my mother or a co-wife leap to gather the crying child in her arms? Was my father anywhere near? I am frustrated because I can not answer the doctor's questions. And I feel him, there behind my head, pen poised to at last capture on paper an African woman's psychosis for the greater glory of his profession. Olivia has brought me here. Not to the father of psychoanalysis, for he has died, a tired, persecuted man. But to one of his sons, whose imitation of him—including dark hair and beard, Egyptian statuettes on his desk, the tribal-rug-covered couch and the cigar, which smells of bitterness—will perhaps cure me.

Olivia

You have to keep us in mind, Tashi would say. And we would laugh, because it was so easy to forget Africa in America. What most people remembered was strange, because unlike the two of us, they had never been there.

Adam

Perhaps it is odd, but I do not recall my first meeting with Tashi. But children don't exactly "meet," do they? Unless it is a formal occasion; which, to think of it, our arrival in Olinka certainly must have been. The villagers were smiling anxiously at us, when we arrived, and were dressed in their colorful and scanty best. There was food cooking in pots and roasting on spits. There was even a warmish melon-flavored drink that made me think, longingly, of lemonade. I noticed the small boys my own age, their knobby knees and shaved heads. Their near nakedness. I noticed the men: the seedlike tribal markings on their cheeks and the greasy amulets they wore around their necks. I noticed the dust and the heat. The flies. I noticed the long flat breasts of the women who worked barebreasted, babies on their backs, as they swept and tidied up the village as if in expectation of inspection. I was too young to be embarrassed by their partial nudity. And so I stared,

13

mouth open, until Mama Nettie poked me firmly in the back with her parasol.

And now when Olivia says, But *don't* you remember, Adam, Tashi was *weeping* when we met her! I am at a loss. For that is not the little girl I remember. The Tashi I remember was always laughing, and making up stories, or flitting cheerfully about the place on errands for her mother.

Sometimes I think Olivia and I remember two entirely different people, and now, because Tashi and I have lived together for so many years, I think my recollection of her as a child is sure to be the correct one. But what if it is not?

Tashi

They were always saying *You mustn't cry!*

These are new people coming to live among us, and to meet them in tears is to bring bad luck to us. They'll think we beat you! Yes, we understand your sister is dead, but . . . time now to put on a good face and make the foreigners welcome. If you can't behave, we will have to ask your mother to take you elsewhere.

How could I believe these were the same women I'd known all my life? The same women who'd known Dura? And whom Dura had known? She'd gone to buy matches or snuff for them nearly every day. She'd carried their water jugs on her head.

It was a nightmare. Suddenly it was not acceptable to speak of my sister. Or to cry for her.

Let us leave here, Mama, I finally said in despair. And my mother, her face stern, took my hand in hers and walked off with me toward our farm.

We stayed there seven weeks; long after our crops had been tended. Besides, there was a boy who lived

15

on the farms who would have looked after our plots if we had decided to go back to the village. But my mother and I stayed, until even the groundnuts had been pulled up, placed on racks—the round ones that from a distance look like little hats—and dried. Then we stripped the nuts from their shriveled yellow stems and carried loads of them home to the village on our backs.

How small I felt, especially since Dura was no longer around to measure myself against. Not there to tease me that I had grown perhaps the thickness of a coin but still had not caught up with her ... And there was my mother, trudging along the path in front of me, her load of groundnuts forcing her nearly double.

I have never seen anyone work as hard as my mother, or pull her share of the work with a more resigned dignity.

Tashi, she would say, it is only hard work that fills the emptiness.

But I had not previously understood her.

Now I watched the backs of her legs and noted how they sometimes quivered with the effort to ascend a steep hill; for there were many hills between our farm and the village. Indeed, the farm was in a completely different climate from that of the village: hot but moist, because there was a river and still a bit of forest, whereas the village was hot and dry, with few trees. I studied the white rinds of my mother's heels, and felt in my own heart the weight of Dura's death settling upon her spirit, like the groundnuts that bent her back. As she staggered under her load, I half expected her footprints, into which I was careful to step, to stain my own feet with tears and blood. But my mother never wept, though like the rest of the women, when called upon to salute the power of the chief and his counselors she could let out a cry that assaulted the very heavens with its praising pain.

Tashi

Negro women, said the doctor, are considered the most difficult of all people to be effectively analyzed. Do you know why?

Since I was not a Negro woman I hesitated before hazarding an answer. I felt negated by the realization that even my psychiatrist could not see I was African. That to him all black people were Negroes.

I had been coming to see him now for several months. Some days I talked; some days I did not. There was a primary school across the street from his office. I would listen to the faint sound of the children playing and often forget where I was, forget why I was there.

He'd been taken aback by the fact that I had only one child. He thought this unusual for a colored woman, married or unmarried. Your people like lots of kids, he allowed.

But how could I talk to this stranger of my lost children? And of how they were lost? One was left speechless by all such a person couldn't know.

18

Negro women, the doctor says into my silence, can never be analyzed effectively because they can never bring themselves to blame their mothers.

Blame them for what? I asked.

Blame them for anything, said he.

It is quite a new thought. And, surprisingly, sets off a kind of explosion in the soft, dense cotton wool of my mind.

But I do not say anything. Those bark-hard, ashen heels trudge before me on the path. The dress above them barely clothing, a piece of rag. The basket of groundnuts suspended from a strap that fits a groove that has been worn into her forehead. When she lifts the basket down, the groove in her forehead remains. On Sundays she will wear her scarf low in an attempt to conceal it. African women like my mother give harsh meaning to the expression "furrowed brow."

Still, the basket itself is lovely and well made, with a red and ochre "sisters elbow" design that no one weaves more neatly than she. That is all I care to think about. But not all that I will.

I did not carry you to term, she has told me, because one day when I was coming back from bathing I was frightened by a leopard. She was acting strangely, and charged me.

I try to imagine a leopard on the path between our farm and the village. Now there are wild dogs and jackals, but nothing so beautiful as a leopard.

M'Lissa came to look after me.

And was I an easy birth?

But she will only look over my head, to the side of my ear. Of course, she murmurs. Of course you were.

19

Alice Walker

Later we discovered someone had shot and skinned her mate and her cubs, my mother sighs.

And that was the official story of my birth.

So that my mind too veered away from myself and my mother's ordeal and went off into the world of the leopard. Soon enough I could see her clearly, licking down her cubs, or having intercourse with her mate. There in the dappled shade of the acacias. Then, the sound of thunder cracking, and all her loved ones down in a flash. And she, to her shame, forced to run away in fear, even as she smelled the blood and saw the bodies sprawled ungracefully. And later, coming back, she would discover all those she loved, just as she'd left them, but stiffly dead and without their skins.

And I could feel the horror in the leopard's heart, and the rage. And now I see a pregnant human appearing on the path, and I leap for her throat.

The other children used to laugh at me. Look at her! they cried. Come see how Tashi has left our world. You can tell because her eyes have glazed over!

20

Tashi

Olivia begged me not to go. But she did not understand.

There was a bird that always cried when friends were parting forever, though the missionaries never believed this. It was called Ochoma, the bird of parting. I heard it as Olivia pleaded with me. I was arrogant, and the Mbeles had sent a captured donkey for me to ride.

I listened to Olivia trying to control her breathing as she held on to the rope bridle. She was crying and there was a part of me that longed to trample her.

She was like a lover.

Tell me to do anything, and I will do it, she said.

Tell me to go anywhere, and I will go, she said.

Only, don't do this to yourself, *please,* Tashi.

The foreigners were so much more melodramatic than Africans ever dared to be. It made one feel contempt for them.

We've been friends almost all our lives, she said. Don't do this to us.

21

She hiccuped, like a child.

Don't do it to Adam.

I had in my mind some outlandish, outsized image of myself. I sat astride the donkey in the pose of a chief, a warrior. We who had once owned our village and hectares and hectares of land now owned nothing. We were reduced to the position of beggars—except that there was no one near enough to beg from, in the desert we were in.

They are right, I said to her from my great height astride the donkey, who say you and your family are the white people's wedge.

She stopped weeping. Wiped her eyes with the back of her hand, and nearly laughed.

Tashi, she said, are you crazy?

I was crazy. For why could I not look at her? I stole glances down alongside her face and let my eyes slide over the top of her head. Her thick hair was braided in two plaits that crossed at the nape of her neck, just as she always wore it. Never would she wear the mealie row fan hairstyle that was traditional with Olinka women.

I had taken off my gingham Mother Hubbard. My breasts were bare. What was left of my dress now rode negligently about my loins. I did not have a rifle or a spear, but I had found a long stick, and with this I jabbed at the ground near her feet.

All I care about now is the struggle for our people, I said. You are a foreigner. Any day you like, you and your family can ship yourselves back home.

Jesus, she said, exasperated.

Also a foreigner, I sneered. I finally looked her in the eye. I hated the way her hair was done.

Who are you and your people never to accept us as we are? Never to imitate any of our ways? It is always we who have to change.

I spat on the ground. It was an expression of contempt only very old Olinkans had known how to use to full effect.

Olivia, who knew the gesture, seemed to wilt, there in the heat.

You want to change us, I said, so that we are like you. And who are *you* like? Do you even know?

I spat in the dust again, though I only made the sound of spitting; my mouth and throat were dry.

You are black, but you are not like us. We look at you and your people with pity, I said. You barely have your own black skin, and it is fading.

I said this because her skin was mahogany while mine was ebony. In happier times I had thought only of how beautiful our arms looked when we, admiring our grass bracelets, held them up together.

But she was suddenly stepping back from the donkey. Her hands at her sides.

I laughed.

You don't even know what you've lost! And the nerve of you, to bring us a God someone else chose for you! He is the same as those two stupid braids you wear, and that long hot dress with its stupid high collar!

Finally, she spoke.

Go, she said, and raised her chin sadly. I did not understand you hated me.

She said it with the quietness of defeat.

I dug my heels into the flanks of the donkey and we trotted out of the encampment. I saw the children, potbellied and with dying eyes, which made them look very wise. I saw the old people laid out in the shade of the rocks, barely moving on their piles of rags. I saw the women making stew out of bones. We had been stripped of everything but our black skins. Here and there a defiant cheek bore the mark of our withered tribe. These marks gave me courage. I wanted such a mark for myself.

My people had once been whole, pregnant with life.

I turned my back on the sister of my heart, and rushed away from her stricken face. I recognized myself as the leopard in her path.

Tashi

And what about your dreams? the doctor one day asks me.

I tell him I do not dream.

I do not dare tell him about the dream I have every night that terrifies me.

Adam

Your wife refuses to talk about her dreams, the doctor says, mysteriously. Above the couch, on which I imagine Evelyn lying, there is a blue, over-arching figure of Nut. The body of woman as night sky. I sit uneasily in my chair, as if I am being interrogated as a spy, my damp palms resting on top of talons that end the chair's arms.

I shrug. I certainly cannot speak of them.

But I am instantly back in our bed, sharing the night and its terrors with my wife. She is upright, clutching her pillow. Her eyes are enormous. She is shaking with fear.

There is a tower, she says. I think it is a tower. It is tall, but I am inside. I don't really ever know what it looks like from outside. It is cool at first, and as you descend lower and lower to where I'm kept, it becomes dank and cold, as well. It's dark. There is an endless repetitive sound that is like the faint scratch of a baby's fingernails on paper. And there are millions of things moving about me in the dark. I

26

can not see them. And they've broken my wings! I see them lying crossed in a corner like discarded oars. Oh, and they're forcing something in one end of me, and from the other they are busy pulling something out. I am long and fat and the color of tobacco spit. Gross! And I can not move!

I did not know I would finally marry Tashi. For many years she was like another sister to me; always about the parsonage, playing with my sister, Olivia, the two of them frequently going on outings with my mother. I teased her mercilessly, and tried to boss her about. Like Olivia, she always stood her ground. I liked her mealie row fan hairstyle and her impish, darting ways. I liked her self-possession. And her passion for storytelling.

We became lovers partly because we were so used to each other.

In Olinka society the strongest taboo was against making love in the fields. So strong was this taboo that no one in living memory had broken it. And yet, we did. And because no one in the society could imagine us capable of such an offense—lovemaking in the fields jeopardized the crops; indeed, it was declared that if there was any fornication whatsoever in the fields the crops definitely would not grow—no one ever saw us, and the fields produced their harvests as before.

I am thinking of our lovemaking, as the doctor waits for more of a response about Evelyn's dreaming.

She dreams they have imprisoned her and broken her wings, I say into the suspense.

They, who? the doctor asks.

But this, I say, I do not know.

She was like a fleshy, succulent fruit; and when I was not with her I dreamed of the time I would next lie on my belly between her legs, my cheeks caressed by the gentle rhythms of her thighs. My tongue bringing us no babies, and to both of us delight. This way of loving, among her people, the greatest taboo of all.

Adam

I could not bear the happiness of my father and aunt, who had decided they would be married during our visit to London. Nor could I stand the solicitude of Olivia, who empathized with me as I thrashed about, missing Tashi, though furious with her. I pounded the streets of London until my feet, in new hard leather shoes, were bruised. Only the weather made the days bearable. It was spring, and the beauty of the city was formidable. There were lilacs everywhere, and the air was filled with the sound of singing birds.

The Missionary Society had put us up in spacious rooms near St. James's Park, and Olivia and I spent hours underneath the ancient trees. We enjoyed watching the men and women who came out of their homes promptly at quarter to four, on their way to tea at other people's homes, and who crossed in front of us, reservedly whispering. My window looked out right into the trees, and there was so much sky I often woke up thinking I was still in Africa.

29

After the wedding, I took the boat train to Paris, hoping that the change of scenery would do me good. There was also a young woman I hoped to see, whose name was Lisette.

Lisette had visited us in Olinka as part of the youth group of her church. We often entertained visitors, from all over the world, and this was rather perfunctory, even predictable and boring, but she and I had struck up a lively conversation about some of her family's experiences as colonialists in Algeria, where she had lived the earlier part of her life, and had had the opportunity to spend several hours alone in each other's company. This was possible because I was then tending an elderly parishioner who lived on the outskirts of the village. There was no one else to feed and clothe him during the last weeks of his life, and so my father had assigned this task to me, in the hope, I suppose, that it would increase my feelings of humility. I was bored to distraction, and actively prayed for my patient to loose his feeble hold on life and die, which he eventually did.

It was to this post, Torabe's hut, that Lisette followed me. She stood by, chestnut-haired and pale, very pretty in the startling white people's way that seems something of a clash at times with natural surroundings, as I fed and washed him and dressed his sores—for he had lain on his rags for a long time—and she chattered on about the charms of Paris. She spoke English with an accent that embellished it.

I could not believe I'd found her so easily. But

soon we were cozily sipping coffee in her tiny doll's
house near the train station, a house that had been
left her by her grandmother, and she was telling me
about her career as a teacher. In her surroundings I
felt it was I who clashed.

But you did not come all this way to hear about
French high school students, she said, passing me a
dainty slice of cake.

You seem troubled, no? What is the use?

It was a minor slip, charming, and made me laugh.
It was just how I felt.

You live alone here, and no one bothers you? I
said.

She shrugged.

And no one cares that you are not married and
that you make your own living?

Mais non, she said. Women are no longer chattel,
she sniffed. Even if it is only very recently that
Frenchwomen got the vote. Now, she said, frowning,
we get to vote for one man after another.

I smiled sadly.

I wanted so much to ask her about her sex life.
When, whether, to whom she made love. How the
act of lovemaking felt to her. Whether she knew and
practiced the ways to make love without making
babies.

I asked instead about her church. Whether she was
still active in it. Whether it still sent youth groups to
Africa.

Well, to tell the truth, she said, I have lost the faith.
I look and look in this religion of mine and I am
nowhere in it. When I was younger I thought the

church was there because it helped everybody enlarge their spirit, but really, people around here appear to be more meanspirited than ever.

She stopped suddenly.

Don't get me started. What happened was I could not reconcile the word "obedience" that the bride says in the church wedding with any kind of spiritual or physical expansion for myself. I felt tricked by that word.

I thought of my father and of Mama Nettie. Had "obey" been a word used in their marriage ceremony? And would Mama Nettie "obey" my father? I knew them well enough to know they'd strive to please each other; they already did so. Neither he nor she would have the last word. But why did the word exist, in a ceremony between equals and loved ones? Well, obviously because the woman, who was required to obey, was not considered equal.

I thought of Tashi. Each time we made love, she'd wanted me as much as I'd wanted her. She had engineered most of our meetings. Whenever we held each other she was breathless in anticipation. Once, she claimed her heart nearly stopped. Such pleasure as ours was difficult for us to believe. Was it a pleasure of which others knew? we often asked ourselves. The faces of our elders in the village bore no hint of it.

PART
TWO

Tashi

Can you bear to know what I have lost? I scream this at the judges, in their stupid white wigs. And at the lawyers—my own and the one hired to prosecute me. They are both young, dapper African men who would not look out of place in London, Paris or New York. I scream it at the curious onlookers for whom my trial is entertainment. But most of all, I scream it at my family: Adam, Olivia, Benny.

No one responds to my question. The prosecuting attorney suppresses a smile because I have lost control. The judges rap their pencils on their tea trays.

But on the morning of the twelfth of October last did you not make a point of buying several razors at the shop near the Ombere bus station?

Once upon a time there was a man with a very long and tough beard . . . I began without thinking. Stopping only when it dawned on me that the entire courtroom had burst into laughter. Even Olivia, when I cast a glance at her, was smiling. Oh, Tashi, her look seemed to say, even here, on trial for your life, you are still making things up!

If you would be so kind as to answer the question, says the dapper young attorney, and not attempt to indulge and distract the court with your fantasy life.

My fantasy life. Without it I'm afraid to exist. Who am I, Tashi, renamed in America "Evelyn," Johnson?

The razor to me was always associated with men, with beards and barber stools. Until I went to America it would never have occurred to me to pick one up, to shave my legs and underarms with it.

Yes, I say to the attorney, I bought three razors.

Why three? he asks.

Because I wanted to be sure.

Sure of what?

To do the job properly.

You mean to kill the old woman?

Yes.

That is all, Your Honors, he says.

That night in my cell I suddenly remembered the large razor I saw at the old man's house in Bollingen, when Adam took me there. It was truly huge, as if it had belonged to a giant. I thought: How could a man's face be so large; it would be almost like shaving one's face with an axe. It was lying outside in the loggia, near the fireplace, and the old man used it, along with a large machete, to shave off slivers of wood for kindling. It was black and ancient, with Chinese dragons engraved in greenish bronze on its sides. The blade was exceedingly sharp. I couldn't keep my eyes off it. The old man, noticing my fascination, placed it tenderly in my hands, closing

36

my fingers over it protectively. It *is* beautiful, isn't it? he asked, but I thought he observed my clutching of the thing with a quizzical look in his eye.

I held the razor and looked out over Lake Zurich. Marveling that after our long trip, Adam and I had indeed arrived there.

We had flown first to London, where Olivia was speaking before the Theosophy Society, and then to Paris, and then on to Zurich, a remarkably clean and somnolent city. In fact, from the airplane window the whole of Switzerland seemed to be quietly sleeping. Everything neat and trim, *safe*. There was an air of thrift, of husbandry, even before one touched the ground. I could see that the forests were carefully tended: where trees were taken out, seedlings were put in. It seemed a country in miniature, where every slight wrong might be corrected, without much trouble.

I remarked to Adam how odd this was: that the people's characteristics, easily discerned, were imprinted on the landscape.

But that is true everywhere, he said. Everywhere some people go they wreck the land, he said. But this is the land of people who've stayed home. Mountains, he said, gesturing at the magnificent Alps, make a wonderful fence.

We were circling the airport. It was in the middle of a field. There were cows and, as we descended closer to the ground, white clover and yellow wildflowers.

There was a train to Bollingen, and we took it. It ran noiselessly on its track, its conductor a redfaced, jovial fellow with graying flaxen hair. We looked out the window at the chalet-style houses, the acres of grapes, the family plots of corn. Gardens everywhere.

I had never imagined a warm Switzerland. In my imagination it was always snowing. People were on skis. The ground was white. There was hot chocolate. To feel the intense heat of the sun, to see people in summer pastels, to glimpse an ice cream vendor in one of the stations, amused me. I felt that my child self, who'd so loved to imagine snowy northern landscapes, especially while I was growing up in equatorial Africa, was experiencing a treat.

Adam seemed somewhat nervous as the train neared the station. Departures and arrivals always upset him. I remembered when we first arrived in America. His excitement to be, finally, "safe" and back home. And his shock at being constantly harassed because he was black.

No, no, he used to correct me. They behave this way not because I'm black but because they are white.

It seemed a curious distinction at the time. I was in love with America. I did not find Americans particularly rude. But then I had not been steeped in the history that Adam's father had insisted he and Olivia study, in preparation for their return home. I felt I was able to see everything in a much more expansive way. For I saw everything fresh, and with wonder that I was in America at all. If a white person was rude I simply turned and stared. I never acknowledged the system that sanctioned rude behavior, but always responded directly to the person.

How uncivilly you have been brought up! was the message of my stare.

We were so intent on reaching the end of our long journey that we missed the station and rode on, oblivious, to the one beyond it, Schmerikon, a pleasant hamlet close to the shore of the lake. Hot and flustered, we clambered down from the train and made our way to a small café just by the station. Adam ordered a sandwich—for we'd had no food all day—and I ordered cheese on a roll, a green salad, and lemonade.

There we sat, in the shade of a linden tree, two rotund black people in advanced middle age, our hair graying, our faces glistening with sweat. We might have been models for a painting by Horace Pippin.

Adam

The first thing I noticed was the flatness of her gaze. It frightened me.

As soon as we returned from England, my aunt and father securely married, I tore off across the country in search of Tashi. It was a long journey that took several months, because I was frequently on foot and had little idea where I was going. During the final month I found myself following a trail whose markers consisted of crossed sticks and odd configurations of rocks piled near watering holes. Then, when I finally dragged my ragged and weary body into the Mbele camp, I was seized by the warriors who stood watch over the encampment, and taken to an isolated compound for interrogation.

Such a possibility—that I might be captured by some of Africa's liberators—had not occurred to me, innocent that I was. I had thought, also, that the Mbeles, if they existed at all, would all speak Olinka, or at least KiSwahili, a smattering of which I knew. But no, these freedom fighters were obviously from

40

different parts of Africa. There was even, I was to
learn later, a European woman, a European man and
several American blacks of both sexes in the camp.
Since my interrogators spoke neither Olinka nor
English, it was a long time, perhaps a week, before I
was able to make them understand I meant no harm
but was merely looking for someone. Even after a
week of sign language and the drawing of figures on
the ground I could see they were not convinced. For
one thing, they were suspicious of my shoes. A pair
of stout English sandals I'd brought from London.
And of course my wristwatch, with its gold Spandex
band, was the kind of luxury item only a white
person, in their opinion and experience, could afford
to wear. I offered to give them both watch and shoes
in exchange for my freedom. But it soon became
clear that if they decided I was indeed harmless, that
is to say, not a spy, they planned to recruit me. Once
I realized this, I rested a bit easier. For I discovered
that, face-to-face with these cold black men, I was
stricken with the most craven fear. They were all
"business." They neither joked among themselves
nor smiled. I had never seen blacks like my captors
before.

There was a flicker in the eye of one of them one
day when I rambled on to them in Olinka. I think it
was the word for water that caused it. In Olinka the
word for water is *barash,* and I was constantly having
to ask them for more. It was hot where we were, in a
canyon surrounded by massive rock cliffs that
soaked up the broiling sun all day long. I felt I would
die of thirst. I knew they resented bringing the heavy
jar of water to my hut. Partly because it was heavy,

and had to be brought a good distance from the river, but also because the carrying of water was not a man's job. It was a woman's job. However, since I was a prisoner, and interrogating a prisoner in strictest secrecy was a man's job, the bringing of the water had also, of necessity, become a man's job.

It was not long after I saw the flicker in the guard's eye that a young man from Olinka was brought to talk to me. He said his name was Banse, and when we'd talked a bit I remembered him slightly. It was really his parents I remembered, for they were staunch Christians and supporters of my father and the church. When last I'd seen Banse he was a small boy. He was still quite young, fifteen or so, with a high square forehead and wary, veiled eyes. He said there were many Olinkans in the camp. Women as well as men. He said of course Tashi was among them, but he believed her to be indisposed.

It was difficult to maintain my composure when I heard this. I clenched my teeth with the effort. It was enough that she was alive, I thought. After the grueling journey, which I had feared I'd never complete, it was nearly impossible to imagine that Tashi, riding her donkey and walking, had survived it as well.

When I had been vouched for by Banse, the manner of my guards immediately changed. Their stiff, absurdly militaristic posture—as if learned from Hitler himself—collapsed into the graceful melted-bones stride of the ordinary unhurried African. They smiled, they joked. They offered me tea.

Tea, they explained, came from the Europeans in the camp, one of whom was a son of the owner of a vast tea plantation that had displaced the homes of a thousand nomadic Africans. Bob, this son, had grown up on the plantation until he was ten, then had been sent to England to boarding school. The only blacks he'd ever seen around their place had been servants.

This was all I learned of Bob, the bringer of tea. I found it bizarre that he knew exactly where they were and had access to their hiding place. Indeed, I was to learn he had his own hut among them and lived in it most of the time.

Good tea! My captors laughed, liberally lacing it with sugar, and toasting me with their overflowing mugs.

The Mbele camp was a replica of an African village, though considerably spread out and camouflaged. No hut was in the open, but rather each was nestled close to the base of large trees or towering rocks. The pens of the animals likewise hugged the base of the cliffs. It was all reminiscent of the ancient settlements of the cliffdwelling Dogonese, photographs of which I had seen. Nothing, however, except a wisp of smoke perhaps, would have indicated human habitation, if one were in a plane looking down from above.

Tashi was in a rough bower made of branches. Lying on a mat made from the grass that grew around the camp. And as she lay there, her head and shoulders propped against a boulder that resembled a small animal, she was busy making more of these grass mats. I could not tell if she was happy to see me. Her eyes no longer sparkled with anticipation. They were as flat as eyes that have been painted in, and with dull paint. There were five small cuts on each side of her face, like the marks one makes to keep score while playing tic-tac-toe. Her legs, ashen and wasted, were bound.

Her first words to me were: You should not be here.

My first words to her were: Where else should I be?

This reply appeared to leave her speechless. While she struggled to control her expression, so revealing of her hurt, I crawled on my knees to where she lay, took her in my arms, and sighed.

Tashi

He has come for me, I thought. He has finally come, God alone knows how. He is ragged and dirty and his hair is that of a savage, or of a crazy person isolated in the bush. He is here. And I can see as he looks at me that he does not know whether to laugh or cry. I feel the same. My eyes see him but they do not register his being. Nothing runs out of my eyes to greet him. It is as if my self is hiding behind an iron door.

I am like a chicken bound for market. The scars on my face are nearly healed, but I must still fan the flies away. The flies that are attracted by the odor coming from my blood, eager to eat at the feast provided by my wounds.

PART
THREE

Evelyn

Yours is the pain of the careless carpenter who, with his hammer, bashes his own thumb, says The Old Man.

He is no longer actively practicing his profession as doctor of the soul. He is seeing me only because I am an African woman and my case was recommended to him by his niece, my husband's friend and lover, the Frenchwoman, Lisette. It is hard for me to think about the conversations Adam and Lisette must have had about me over the years, on his twice-yearly visits to Paris and her annual visit to California. Often, while she is visiting, I have had to be sedated. On occasion I have voluntarily checked myself into the Waverly Psychiatric Hospital, in which, because it is run by a man affiliated with Adam's ministry, I am always given a room.

I liked The Old Man immediately. Liked his great, stooping height; the looseness of the ever-present tweed jacket that hung from his gaunt shoulders. Liked his rosy pink face and small blue eyes that looked at one so piercingly it was difficult not to turn one's head to see what he was viewing through it. Liked, even, that he himself had at times a look of madness to match my own—though it was a benign look that seemed to observe a connection between whatever held his gaze and some grand, unimaginably spacious design, quite beyond one's comprehension. In other words, he looked as if he would soon die. I found this comforting.

Adam

At first she merely spoke about the strange compulsion she sometimes experienced of wanting to mutilate herself. Then one morning I woke to find the foot of our bed red with blood. Completely unaware of what she was doing, she said, and feeling nothing, she had sliced rings, bloody bracelets, or chains, around her ankles.

Evelyn

I did not fear him partly because I did not fear his house. Though medieval European in its outer aspects, particularly its turrets and small slate courtyard, it had at its center a stone hut, round, with a large fireplace and flagstone hearth. He knelt there, his old knees creaking, to light the morning and evening fire, over which he cooked; and seemed to me, at times, an old African grandmother, metamorphosed somehow into a giant pinkfaced witchdoctor on this other, colder continent. He almost always wore an apron of some kind. Of leather, when he chopped wood or carved the stone pillars that stood near the lake across from the loggia, or a thick cotton one when he cooked the wonderful Swiss pancakes and sausages with which he delighted to feed us.

His hair was as wispy and pale as thistle; I would sometimes, late in our visit, creep up behind him— as he sat smoking with Adam and looking out over the lake—and blow it. This caused him to reach up behind him, grasp both my arms, pull me forward against his large back and shoulders, hug me to him with my head like a moon above his own, and laugh.

We used to tell him, Adam and I, *Mzee* (Old Man), you are our last hope!

But he would only look from one to the other of us—a grave look—and in his heavily accented English he would say, No, that is not correct. You yourselves are your last hope.

Evelyn

He set me to drawing. The first thing I drew was the meeting of my mother and the leopard on her path. For this, after all, represented my birth. My entrance into reality. But I drew, then painted, a leopard with two legs. My terrified mother with four.

Why is this? asked The Old Man.

I did not know.

Evelyn

Benny tells me there is a lot of discussion now in the newspapers and on the street about whether, since I've been an American citizen for years, the Olinka government even has the right to put me on trial. He thinks there is a possibility I'll be extradited back to the United States. He sits tensely, reading me notes he has made on the subject.

Sometimes I dream of the United States. I love it deeply and miss it terribly, much to the annoyance of some people I know. In all my dreams there is clear rushing river water and flouncy green trees, and where there are streets they are wide and paved and in the night of my dreams there are lighted windows way above the street; and behind these windows I know people are warm and squeaky clean and eating meat. Safe. I awake here to the odor of unwashed fear, and the traditional porridge and fruit breakfast that hasn't changed since I left. Except my dishes are fresh and appetizingly prepared, thanks to Olivia,

55

Alice Walker

who has made herself welcome, through bribery, in the prison kitchen.

And if I am extradited to America, I say, will I have a second trial?

Benny says he does not know for sure, checking his notes, but that he thinks so. He is tall and gangly, a radiant brown, usually. At the moment, fear has dulled him.

To go through all of this again in America doesn't appeal to me.

The crime they say I committed would make no sense in America. It barely makes sense here.

Evelyn-Tashi

The obstetrician broke two instruments trying to make an opening large enough for Benny's head. Then he used a scalpel. Then a pair of scissors used ordinarily to sever cartilage from bone. All this he told me when I woke up, a look of horror lingering on his face. A look he tried to camouflage by joking.

How did that big baby (Benny was nine pounds) even get up in there, Mrs. Johnson? That's what I'd like to know. He grinned, as if he'd never heard of the aggressive mobility of sperm. I attempted a smile I was incapable of feeling, first in his direction and then down at the baby in my arms. His head was yellow and blue and badly misshapen. I had no idea how to shape it properly, but hoped that once the doctor left, instinct would teach me. Nor could I imagine asking him for any instructions at all.

Adam stood beside the bed, too embarrassed to

speak. He coughed whenever he was embarrassed or nervous; now he cleared his throat repeatedly. With my free hand, I reached for him. He moved closer, but did not touch me; the sound in his throat causing my own to close. After a moment, I withdrew my hand.

Tashi-Evelyn

I felt as if there was a loud noise of something shattering on the hard floor, there between me and Adam and our baby and the doctor. But there was only a ringing silence. Which seemed oddly, after a moment, like the screaming of monkeys.

Tashi-Evelyn

So this is how there could have been an immaculate conception, he'd said bitterly, when I told him I was pregnant; meaning it literally, Bible scholar that he was. After three months of trying, he had failed to penetrate me. Each time he touched me I bled. Each time he moved against me I winced. There was nothing he could do to me that did not hurt. Still, somehow, I became pregnant with Benny. Having experienced the pain of getting Benny "up in there," we were terrorized waiting for his birth.

No matter how sick I became during the pregnancy, I attended myself. I could not bear the thought of the quick-stepping American nurses looking at me as if I were some creature from beyond their imaginings. In the end, though, I was that creature. For even as I gave birth, a crowd of nurses, curious hospital staff and medical students gathered around my bed. For days afterward doctors and nurses from around the city and for all I know around the state came by to peer over the shoulder of my doctor as he examined me. There was also the question of what to do with "the hole," as I overheard him call it, making no attempt to be euphemistic for my sake.

At last Adam put a stop to the sideshow my body had become and for the last three days in the hospital I held Benny close, gently and surreptitiously stroking his head into more normal contours (work I instinctively felt should be done with my tongue); or, when the nurse had taken him away, I turned my face to the wall and slept. I slept so long and so hard it was always necessary for the nurse to shake me when it was time for a feeding.

My doctor sewed me up again, much as I'd been fastened originally, because otherwise there would have been a yawning unhealable wound. But it was done in such a way that there was now room for pee and menstrual blood more easily to pass. The doctor said that now, also, after giving birth, I could have intercourse with my husband.

Benny, my radiant brown baby, the image of Adam, was retarded. Some small but vital part of his brain crushed by our ordeal. But thankfully, during the period I spent in hospital, and even for years afterward, I did not recognize this.

Adam

They had dug out a little hole in the dirt beneath her, and that was her personal latrine.

She was on her moons when I arrived, there was only one old woman, M'Lissa, from Olinka, to help her, and there were flies, and a slight but unmistakable odor.

M'Lissa grumbled about the lack of everything. In the old days, she said, Tashi would have wanted for nothing. There would have been a score of maidens initiated with her, and their mothers, aunts and older sisters would have taken charge of the cooking (important because there were special foods one ate at such a time that kept the stools soft, thus eliminating some of the pain of evacuation), the cleaning of the house, the washing, oiling and perfuming of Tashi's body.

I had never spoken to M'Lissa other than to say hello. I knew from Tashi that M'Lissa had brought her into the world. I knew that, among the Olinka, she was a prized midwife and healer, though to those

Christianized ones who also turned to Western medicine, she was shunned. I was surprised to see her in the Mbele camp. More because she was old, and limped, than for any other, more ideological, reason. How had she, dragging her lame foot, dressed in rags, come so far from home?

It was only in the late afternoons that she could talk, arriving breathless after a day of tending others in the camp, as she shifted Tashi and washed and oiled her wound, which she invariably referred to not as a wound but as a healing. She told me she had at first been in a refugee camp over the border from Olinka; a horrible place, she said, filled with dying Olinkans who fled the fighting between the Mbele rebels and the white government's troops, most of whom were members of the black minority tribes that hated the dominant Olinkans. They had been cruel beyond anything she'd ever seen, specializing in hacking off the limbs of their captives. In the camp she had been in demand, though she'd had nothing beyond her two hands to work with. There had been no herbs, no oils, no antiseptics, not even water at times. She had delivered babies in the dark, set bones, and used stones to smooth the protruding gristle of amputated limbs. There was nothing to assist her beyond her patients' grim endurance. It was in the refugee camp, she said, that her hair turned completely white, and where, eventually, she lost it. Now, she said, running a gnarled hand back and forth over it in self-derision, I am as bald as an egg.

The other women in the camp, according to M'Lissa, had all been initiated at the proper age.

63

Either shortly after birth, or at the age of five or six, but certainly by the onset of puberty, ten or eleven. She had argued with Catherine, Tashi's mother, to have the operation done for Tashi when she too was at the proper age. But, because Catherine had gone Christian, she'd turned a deaf ear to her. Now, M'Lissa said, with a grimace of justification, it was the grownup daughter who had come to her, wanting the operation because she recognized it as the only remaining definitive stamp of Olinka tradition. And of course, now, she added, Tashi would not have the shame of being unmarried.

I wanted to marry her, I said.

You are a foreigner, she said, dismissing me.

I still want to marry her, I said, taking Tashi's hand.

M'Lissa seemed confused. Nothing in her experience had prepared her for a possibility such as this.

I never saw the other women in the camp. M'Lissa told us they were all on missions of liberation. Tashi said she thought it was the women's task to forage for food and to conduct raids against the plantations, most of them now left in the hands of loyal African retainers. A primary use of these raids was to recruit new warriors to swell the ranks of the Mbele rebels.

The operation she'd had done to herself joined her, she felt, to these women, whom she envisioned as strong, invincible. Completely woman. Completely African. Completely Olinka. In her imagination, on her long journey to the camp, they had seemed terribly bold, terribly revolutionary and free. She saw them leaping to the attack. It was only when she at last was told by M'Lissa, who one day unbound her legs, that she might sit up and walk a few steps that she noticed her own proud walk had become a shuffle.

It now took a quarter of an hour for her to pee. Her menstrual periods lasted ten days. She was incapacitated by cramps nearly half the month. There were premenstrual cramps: cramps caused by the near impossibility of flow passing through so tiny an aperture as M'Lissa had left, after fastening together the raw sides of Tashi's vagina with a couple of thorns and inserting a straw so that in healing, the traumatized flesh might not grow together, shutting the opening completely; cramps caused by the residual flow that could not find its way out, was not reabsorbed into her body, and had nowhere to go. There was the odor, too, of soured blood, which no amount of scrubbing, until we got to America, ever washed off.

Olivia

It was heartbreaking to see, on their return, how passive Tashi had become. No longer cheerful, or impish. Her movements, which had always been graceful, and quick with the liveliness of her personality, now became merely graceful. Slow. Studied. This was true even of her smile; which she never seemed to offer you without considering it first. That her soul had been dealt a mortal blow was plain to anyone who dared look into her eyes.

Adam brought her home to us just as we were about to leave for America. He married her, our father presiding, even as she protested that, in America, he would grow ashamed of her because of the scars on her face. The evening before the wedding, Adam had these same Olinka tribal markings carved into his own cheeks. His handsome face was swollen; his smile, because of the pain involved, impossible. No one spoke of the other, the hidden scar, between Tashi's thin legs. The scar that gave her the classic Olinka woman's walk, in which the feet appear to slide forward and are rarely raised above the ground. No one mentioned the eternity it took her to use the w.c. No one mentioned the smell.

In America, we solved the problem of cleaning behind the scar by using a medical syringe that looked like a small turkey baster, and this relieved Tashi of an embarrassment so complete she had taken to spending half the month completely hidden from human contact, virtually buried.

PART
FOUR

Tashi

On very warm days The Old Man took us sailing on his boat, up and down and all around Lake Zurich. His ruddy face eager before so much sun, his large hands moving deftly in a contest with tide and wind. His age suddenly amounting to no more than his head of wispy white hair. I would stand hugging the mast, or else sit low in the boat and feel the spray cool and refreshing on my skin.

The Old Man and even Adam seemed mesmerized by my absorption in the water of the lake, which was to me a small sea. I felt their eyes on me, approvingly.

Ja, The Old Man would say to Adam. Your wife is *glow*ing.

Ja, I thought to myself. Perhaps that is a good sign.

Tashi-Evelyn

At night The Old Man played music for us. Music from Africa, India, Bali. He had an amazing record collection that occupied one wall of his house. He showed us grainy black-and-white films, made on his trips. It was during the showing of one of these films that something peculiar happened to me. He was explaining a scene in which there were several small children lying in a row on the ground. He thought, first of all, that they were boys, which I could see straight off they were not, though their heads were shaved and they each wore a scanty loincloth. He assumed, he said, he had inadvertently interrupted a kind of ritual ceremony having to do with the preparation of these children for adulthood. Everything, in any case, had stopped, the moment he and his entourage entered the ritual space. And what was also odd, he said, was how no one spoke a word, or even moved, as long as he and his people were there. They literally froze as the camera panned the area.

The children on the ground in a little row, lying close together on their backs, the adults simply stopped in midactivity, unmoving, even, it appeared, unseeing. Only—he laughed, relighting his pipe, which had gone out, as it frequently did, while he talked—there was a large fighting cock (which we now saw as it stepped majestically into the frame) and it walked about quite freely, crowing mightily (it was a silent film but we could certainly perceive its exertions), and that was the only sound or movement while we were there.

The film ran on, but suddenly I felt such an overwhelming fear that I fainted. Quietly. Slid off my chair and onto the bright rug that covered the stone floor. It was exactly as if I had been hit over the head. Except there was no pain.

When I came to, I was in the guest bedroom upstairs in the turret. Adam and the old man were bending over me. There was nothing I could tell them; I could not say, The picture of a fighting cock, taken twenty-five years ago, completely terrorized me. And so I laughed off my condition and said it was caused by too much happiness, sailing in the high altitude.

The Old Man looked skeptical and did not seem surprised when, the next afternoon, I began to paint what became a rather extended series of ever larger and more fearsome fighting cocks.

And then one day, into the corner of my painting, there appeared, I drew, a foot. Sweating and shivering as I did so. Because I suddenly realized there was something, some small thing the foot was holding between its toes. It was for this small thing that the giant cock waited, crowing impatiently, extending its neck, ruffling its feathers, and strutting about.

There are no words to describe how sick I felt as I painted. How nauseous; as the cock continued to grow in size, and the bare foot with its little insignificant morsel approached steadily toward what I felt would be the crisis, the unbearable moment, for me. For, as I painted, perspiring, shivering, and moaning faintly, I felt that every system in my body, every connecting circuit in my brain, was making an effort to shut down. It was as if the greater half of my being were trying to murder the lesser half, and as I painted—by now directly onto the wall of the bedroom, because only there could I paint the cock as huge as it now appeared to be: it dwarfed me—I dragged the brush to paint each towering iridescent green feather, each baleful gold fleck in its colossal red and menacing eye.

The foot grew large too. But not nearly as large as the cock.

When The Old Man looked at it he said: Well, Evelyn, is it a man's foot or a woman's foot?

The question puzzled me so profoundly I could not answer, but only held my head between my hands in the classic pose of the deeply insane.

A man's foot? A woman's foot?

How could one know?

But then later, in the middle of the night, I found myself painting a design called "crazy road," a pattern of crisscrosses and dots that the women made with mud on the cotton cloth they wove in the village when I was a child. And I suddenly knew that the foot above which I painted this pattern was a woman's, and that I was painting the lower folds of one of M'Lissa's tattered wraps.

As I painted I remembered, as if a lid lifted off my brain, the day I had crept, hidden in the elephant grass, to the isolated hut from which came howls of pain and terror. Underneath a tree, on the bare ground outside the hut, lay a dazed row of little girls, though to me they seemed not so little. They were all a few years older than me. Dura's age. Dura, however, was not among them; and I knew instinctively that it was Dura being held down and tortured inside the hut. Dura who made those inhuman shrieks that rent the air and chilled my heart.

Abruptly, inside, there was silence. And then I saw M'Lissa shuffle out, dragging her lame leg, and at first I didn't realize she was carrying anything, for it was so insignificant and unclean that she carried it not in her fingers but between her toes. A chicken—a hen, not a cock—was scratching futilely in the dirt between the hut and the tree where the other girls, their own ordeal over, lay. M'Lissa lifted her foot and flung this small object in the direction of the hen, and she, as if waiting for this moment, rushed toward M'Lissa's upturned foot, located the flung object in the air and then on the ground, and in one quick movement of beak and neck, gobbled it down.

Adam

Dearest Lisette,

How much I would like to see you, to hold you, to hear your wise words. All night long I have not slept, and I am writing outside in the loggia by the light of a candle, just as the sun is rising over the lake. It is so beautiful here, and so peaceful! Sometimes Evelyn and I are able to enjoy it, along with the agreeable conversation of your charming uncle. At least the two of them get along. As you know, I had feared they would not; Evelyn does not take easily to doctors of any sort, and has, over the years, tended to leave her therapists prostrate in her wake.

As you suggested, the fact that I am here with her, and that this is an isolated, quiet and beautiful spot, seems to calm her. She seems also to like the fact that your uncle is old. She is sometimes merry just at the sight of him, and thinks of him, I believe, as a kind of Santa Claus. As such, he is another representative of the exotic Western and European culture she so adores.

But why, I can hear you wondering, am I up at this hour, and have been up all night? I will tell you. A few nights ago, while your uncle was showing some of his old films of his trip to East Africa—the ones that mesmerized you as a youngster and were the impetus behind your trip to Africa, where we met . . . ! Anyway, he was showing these films to us after a day of picnicking and sailing as far south as Schmerikon and as far north as Kusnacht. We'd feasted, when we arrived back at the house, on a fine dinner of roast pork and potatoes that your uncle had managed to leave cooking for us in the old fireless cooker left to him by his grandmother— perhaps, this fireless cooker, the most intriguing example of his magic, as far as Evelyn is concerned! To be brief, near the end of one of these films, she fainted, her body rigid as death, her teeth clenched in a fierce grimace and, most strange of all, her eyes open. So of course we thought for a moment she'd died. When she came to later she tried to laugh the whole thing off and said she wasn't used to so much activity—sailing and walking and eating—in the unfamiliar altitude.

Though we have a room in a hotel in Schmerikon, we sometimes spend the night with your uncle, especially when he and Evelyn are working particularly well together, and so we stayed the night in the guest bedroom the night this happened. Evelyn slept badly. In the morning she rose early and began, even before breakfast, to paint.

She began to paint a chicken. Over and over. On larger and larger paper. She grew frenzied as the size of the paper she held in her hand seemed to shrink in comparison to the monstrous bird she had in her mind. Then there was the question of how to blend the paints she had—which your uncle had kindly given her—to make something she called a black chromium green. She was frantic to manufacture this color, and this color alone, for the tail feathers of the beast. Her mood was impatient, foul, as she tore the smaller drawings into bits and tore her hair as well, all the while oblivious to the presence of your uncle, who sat on a canvas chair out by the lake, reading, or pretending to; or of my distracted attempts to repair a broken pot that I'd noticed tossed in a corner near the hearth. It looked pre-Columbian, and I handled the shards, and the glue, carefully.

Abruptly, she left us, taking her paints and brushes along. There was a loud snap as she closed the shutter of the upstairs bedroom. And then there was quiet. Only the lapping of the water, the chirping of birds, the rustle of wind in the trees. I fixed the pot, as well as I could do considering a third of it was missing. The Old Man's book now rested on his knees; he was sound asleep.

When night came, I avoided going up to bed. All seemed quiet up there, and I did not want to cause any disturbance; I hoped Evelyn had yielded to exhaustion and drifted into one of her deep, coma-like sleeps that could last for days. But when I finally found myself on the stairs, I noticed a light underneath our door. Opening the door, I was confronted with Evelyn, still busily painting, after twelve hours or more! And now painting a humongous feathered creature—for it was too menacing and evil to be given the simple appellation of chicken or cock—

directly onto your uncle's formerly pristine white walls.

She looked about to drop. But, hearing me enter, she turned and stared. Unseeing, certainly, for she neither spoke nor acknowledged me further. Merely whirled back to her monstrous painting, and appeared to fling herself at it.

I was chilled to the bone. Not only by the wild, ill, distraught look of her; I was used to that; but by the damage she was doing, uncaring, to your uncle's house, and by the painting itself. I did not know its meaning to her, of course, but even without knowing it, I felt the evil she was encountering deep in my own soul.

So, Lisette, that is why I am up so early after a sleepless night.

I trust you are well and that you will continue to write to me care of your uncle. Your letters sustain and comfort me, as they have all these years. I count it the great blessing of my life to be able to call you friend.

Yours,
Adam

Tashi

When at last I completed my painting of "The Beast," as the three of us would subsequently refer to it, my mind and body were beyond exhaustion. I fell backward onto the bed and slept. It was late evening of another day when I awoke to the sound of the wind in the trees, the waves of the lake lapping the shore, and the muted sound of voices. I felt no inclination to stir. I lay as I had fallen, merely turning apprehensive eyes slowly left, toward the wall, to look fully into the wicked gaze of my creature. It no longer frightened me. Indeed, I felt as if I were seeing the cause of my anxiety itself for the first time, exactly as it was. The cock was undeniably overweening, egotistical, puffed up, and it was his diet of submission that had made him so.

I gazed at the foot. Lame, subservient, mindless—as if disconnected from the body of the woman above it. M'Lissa. Here the serenity of my mind sharply decreased. I felt my emotions surge painfully toward the hem of her wrapper. Overcome with grief, I shifted my tearfilled gaze at just the moment Adam's handsome head appeared at the door, followed by Mzee, who carried a tray.

They brought oxtail soup, rye bread, carrot sticks, a sprig of parsley, a cup of warm cider and a bouquet of flowers. They propped me up in bed with gentleness and a mildly expectant air. As I ate they entertained me by telling of the culinary adventure they'd had preparing the meal. The Old Man had concocted the soup, from his memory of his mother's recipe; Adam had made the bread. The parsley, carrots and flowers were from the garden behind the house. Mzee apologized for the woodiness of the carrots that had been left in the earth too long; but I enjoyed them best of all. Their fibrousness scrubbed and refreshed my mouth in a coolly resistant, pleasant way.

I must apologize for all this, I said, indicating my beast.

It is certainly large, said Adam. He was quiet after saying this, because he knew the two of us would talk later.

You must not apologize, said Mzee. He looked at it close up, then turned and walked to a chair by the window across the room. From there he looked at it again.

Remarkable, he said, after nearly an hour contemplating it.

He came forward, finally, and took the tray. I had eaten everything, and this pleased him. He was wearing one of his cotton aprons, and there were signs of his soup-making from his mother's recipe all over it. A small bloodstain glowed maroon near his waist. I looked at it calmly. I had been afraid of the sight of blood for such a long time. And then there had been a period when, if I cut myself, whether accidentally or on purpose, I didn't notice it.

This is the way I should have been working all along, said Mzee, as if to himself, after Adam had left us. Healing is not a bourgeois profession. Sighing deeply, he sat next to me on the bed and reached for my hand.

The silvery blackness of my hand against the parchment rosiness of his was pretty. He looked at our hands thoughtfully for a moment.

I am curious about something, he said.

Ja? I said, in my fake Swiss accent, which always tickled him. Except for The Old Man, I thought the Swiss sounded quite unintelligent when they spoke. But perhaps that is because the rest of the world pokes fun at them for their peculiar accent and curious yodeling. Anyhow, I liked to say *ja*. It sounded ridiculous in my mouth and made Mzee smile.

He was searching now for his pipe, which stuck out of the breast pocket of his apron.

Are you better for having done it? he asked, finding and lighting his pipe. Do you feel better in yourself?

Immeasurably, I said without hesitation. The tears that had evaporated at Mzee's and Adam's appearance now drained heavily from my chin. By the time I finished painting it, I continued in a steady voice, quite as though I were not weeping, I remembered my sister Dura's . . . my sister Dura's . . . I could get no further. There was a boulder lodged in my throat. My heart surged pitifully. I knew what the boulder was; that it was a word; and that behind that word I would find my earliest emotions. Emotions that had frightened me insane. I had been going to say, before the boulder barred my throat: my sister's death; because that was how I had always thought of Dura's demise. She'd simply died. She'd bled and bled and bled and then there was death. No one was responsible. No one to blame. Instead, I took a deep breath and exhaled it against the boulder blocking my throat: I remembered my sister Dura's *murder,* I said, exploding the boulder. I felt a painful stitch throughout my body that I knew stitched my tears to my soul. No longer would my weeping be separate from what I *knew.* I began to wail, there in Mzee's old arms. After a long time, he dried my face, stroked my hair, and comforted me with a motherly squeeze that coincided with each of my hiccups, as my weeping subsided.

They did not know I was hiding in the grass, I said. They had taken her to the place of initiation; a secluded, lonely place that was taboo for the uninitiated. Not unlike the place you showed us in your film.

Ah, said Mzee.

She has been screaming in my ears since it happened, I said, suddenly feeling weary beyond expression.

The Old Man was relighting his pipe, which seemed to have been doused by my tears.

Only I could not hear her, I sighed.

You didn't dare, said The Old Man.

I did not understand him; yet what he said somehow made sense.

He stroked my forehead thoughtfully, got up quietly and left me to the continuation of a very long sleep.

Mzee

Dear Lisette,

No one has called me *Mzee* since the natives of Kenya did so spontaneously over a quarter of a century ago. Even then my hair was graying, my back beginning to stoop. I wore glasses. And yet, somehow I felt it was something other than my age that they were noting, when they called me "The Old Man." Some quality of gravity or self-containment that they recognized. Perhaps I flatter myself, as whites do when blacks offer them a benign label for something characteristically theirs, but which they themselves have failed to acknowledge; deep in our hearts perhaps we expect only vilification; the name "devil," to say the least. It used to amaze me that, wherever I lectured, anywhere in the world, the one sentence of mine which every person of color appreciated and rose to thank me for was "Europe is the mother of all evil," and yet they shook my European hand, smiled warmly into my eyes, and some of them actually patted me on the back. The Africans

85

chose names for us that were suggested to them by our behavior. "Impatient" became the name of a colleague who was always hurrying. "Eats a Lot," the name of the greediest of our crew. "Night Moon," they called the blackest man in their own group, and, indeed, it was the brightness of his blackness that one saw.

It is a new experience having a patient staying across the hall from me, in my own house. In my own retreat! The secret place *I* come to heal myself. Only your entreaties could have gotten me into this. Yet now that Adam and Evelyn are here, it is as if they were meant to be here from the beginning. Sometimes, when I am sitting outside by the lake and happen to glance into the gloom of the house, at just the moment Evelyn is looking out, I am struck by the rightness of seeing her black face at *my* window. Watching Adam attempt to fix the spring in the grandfather clock, as he sits in a flood of sunlight on my doorstep, awakens in me a yearning that is practically a memory.

They, in their indescribable suffering, are bringing me home to something in myself. I am finding myself in them. A self I have often felt was only halfway at home on the European continent. In my European skin. An ancient self that thirsts for knowledge of the experiences of its ancient kin. Needs this knowledge, and the feelings that come with it, to be whole. A self that is horrified at what was done to Evelyn, but recognizes it as something that is also done to me. A truly universal self. That is the essence of healing that in my European, "professional" life I frequently lost.

In any event, I must ask Evelyn why she does not seem to fear *my* turret/*tower*, and what she would say to the gift of a very large bag of clay!

Yours in wonder,
Your uncle Carl

PART
FIVE

Olivia

The prison to which Tashi was taken was built during the colonial period, some thirty years before independence. It was old even before it was made, as African-American Southerners of a certain age say about Death. It was built on the "native" side of town at a time when the town was quite small. A few short streets of stucco houses built in the Victorian plantation style—with deep, shady verandahs—around a small central square where, one imagines, white ladies in silk dresses and carrying matching parasols endlessly paraded. What else was there for them to do, having conceived and then reproduced the master of the house? There is, in fact, running diagonally across from the park in the direction of the more imposing houses, a passageway that is still called White Ladies Lane, though few white people of any sort, other than tourists, stroll on it now. The houses are used as offices by government officials and civil servants. In the early days, just after Independence, black people moved into them but moved out again, as soon as they were able to construct larger and more private compounds further out from the town, which was already becoming a hodgepodge of a typical African city. White Ladies Lane, for instance, soon led not to an immaculately kept (by African peons) park used only for strolling or sunning one's pale offspring, but to the market, with its colorful, ramshackle stalls, smoky braziers from which appetizing aromas arose, vendors hawking their wares in a cacophony of persuasive voices, and the squeal of resistant small animals being sold for matter-of-fact slaughter.

One side of the prison, from a distance, looks down on this, over the rooftops of several rows of shanties and the row of government offices. One reason it had been built on a hill, according to the legend about it that, in the earliest postcolonial days, had been posted near the entrance but was now barely decipherable from age, was because it was also a garrison and command post designed to intimidate and to actively suppress any uprising among the Africans. There had been bunkers around its base, and artillery stations, right in amongst the dusty shrubbery, bougainvillea, jacaranda and hibiscus blossoms.

I had never even seen the prison before I went with Adam to visit Tashi. From outside, its formerly white exterior now streaked with brown, with patches of gray cement and bits of black girders poking through at the corners, many of its windows broken or gone entirely, it hardly seemed habitable. And of course it really was not. Still, it was crammed to the rafters with prisoners. All sizes, all shapes, all ages. Both sexes. One left the comparative silence of the street and immediately encountered a wall of noise. And stench. The second floor had been turned over to a mounting number of AIDS victims, sent to the prison rather than to hospital because the hospital, being small, was swamped. For almost a year the government had said no such thing as AIDS existed in the country; now its presence was acknowledged grudgingly, though there was no official speculation about what might have caused it printed in the news. There was no noise whatsoever from this floor, as men, women and children, all stricken, dragged themselves about, attending each other, or else lay quietly, so emaciated as to appear already dead, on straw mats on the floor. When we looked in, no one appeared to notice.

As we ascended the steps to the third floor, I turned to Adam and said, attempting a joke, *I want to go home.*

So do we all, he replied, grimly, with the downcast, helpless look of a man bound to a woman and to circumstances perpetually beyond his control.

Bentu Moraga
(Benny)

It is only money that changes anything or makes anything happen, I said to my mother, glancing at my notes.

You mustn't think that, she said, gazing out the window. It's so New African.

But look at what you have here, I said, gesturing at the freshly painted walls of her cell. Her bright red plastic chair, her desk, writing materials and books.

I can't be guilt-tripped, she said, smiling. I'm already in prison.

I smiled with her. I liked the person my mother was in prison. She was warm and comfortable, as if she were an entirely different person than the driven, frowning mother I'd always known.

Not many of the other prisoners have a private cell, I said.

No, she agreed. Only the bigwigs who will soon buy their way out and escape punishment altogether. She frowned, and for a moment looked like her other self.

We heard the bigwigs down at the other end of the corridor. All day long they played cards, kept their radios blaring and drank beer. Unlike my mother's, their cells were never locked, and so they visited each other far into the night. They would sometimes visit us, and bring my mother an occasional beer, which she accepted.

I had not understood "bigwig" until I saw the judges at my mother's trial. Sure enough, they wore huge white wigs, with curls at the sides and a queue down the back. My mother laughed at them, which I thought they certainly noticed and which I felt sure they'd punish her for. I wrote a note to myself about this as I sat observing the proceedings in the courtroom.

There are a lot of things I can't do—drive a car, for instance—or even think about. I used to feel there was something mysterious about the way I could never quite keep up in school. I almost made it, but then there would come a point at which I felt myself literally slipping back down the slope. It was a relief, finally, to have it explained to me—not by my mother or my father but by a teacher—that I was a bit retarded, something to do with memory, which meant that just as some people are tall and some are short, some people can think longer or shorter thoughts than others. Not to worry! said my teacher, Miss MacMillan, laughing. You have the attention span of the average American TV viewer. And so I was spared the feeling of being, as my father phrased it, negatively unique.

And yet, there were times when I wished I could remember the name of something for which my mother sent me to the store. I wished I could do without the lists. A list for the market. A list for school. A list of what things to take and bring back from an afternoon of playing in a neighbor's yard. A list of street names by which to steer myself home. Nothing that I was asked to do stayed in my mind. Nor could I even remember I'd been asked. Only the look of exasperation on my mother's face held my attention, but only for a moment. Then I forgot even that.

One of my mother's favorite expressions was: It's a wonder you don't forget I'm your mother! But I never did. Perhaps it was because I felt connected to her scent. Which was warm, lovely, *soft*. I felt I could quite happily have spent my lifetime under one of her arms. This, however, I never mentioned because I sensed it would offend her. My mother bathed constantly, as if to rid herself of any scent whatsoever; to her an agreeable odor was that of Palmolive soap, Pond's cold cream or Nivea lotion. To smell like herself seemed beyond her ability to accept. Even now, in middle age, I like to snuggle her, though contorting my lanky body into a shape that fits cuddly under her neck is something of a feat. She barely tolerates it, though, and immediately moves away.

If I want to talk to her or to my father about anything, I have to write notes about the subject to myself. I have to practice what I want to say and how I want to say it. As others might prepare for an exam whose subject matter is unknown to them, so I must study, cram, for every conversation with my folks.

Adam

It was summer, and we sat on chaises longues under the linden trees in the garden behind Lisette's house. Lisette was knitting gossamer blue wool in the heat, and I made the comment that changed my life forever.

It is so hot, I said, to be knitting wool. Unless, I added, smiling at her, you are expecting to have very cold feet this winter.

Very cold *petits* feet, she said, without looking up.

And that is how I learned of petit Pierre.

I had always been careful with Lisette. More often than not, when we were making love, I did not penetrate her. Ours was a friendship of shared sadness as well as passion, but a friendship first of all, and I spent many nights in her fluffy white bed, holding her in my arms, but so distraught about my own life with Evelyn, all I could yearn for was sleep.

On the other hand, there had been an occasional weak moment, which is, after all, all one needs.

You won't have it, of course, I said.

Lisette's neck, which I referred to sometimes in jest as her thick French neck, grew visibly enlarged. It was the clearest sign of her rage, which she went to great intellectual pains to disguise. It was a stubborn neck, the kind Joan of Arc must have had, and now, looking at me but at the same time rather to one side of me, I saw it and her whole upper body, beneath the sheerness of her white summer dress, flush crimson.

It was not your affair, she said, knitting furiously, a bead of sweat running toward the corner of her limpid brown eye. In her anger, she looked a bit as I imagined Madame Defarge would have, had someone sat in front of her and blocked her view of the guillotine.

Not my . . . I couldn't finish. I looked at her, speechless.

Perhaps it isn't even yours, she said. Perhaps I have a lover, or several, during the months we are apart and you are with your crazy wife in America.

This was not her usual way of referring to Evelyn. I was hurt by it.

The silence that fell between us was rendered somehow ridiculous by the energetic droning of her neighbor's bees, passing in and out of their wooden hives; they made the honey that sweetened our coffee and tea; our empty cups exuded the odor of their work. It was a sound that said so clearly: Life goes on. The pain of it so sure. The sweetness of it so mysterious. It is irrelevant to us that you fight. You might both turn to stone there, and it would only mean our liberation into your garden as well as into our own.

It is mine, I said at last.

Yes, she said, putting down her knitting. But it is more mine than yours.

When? I asked. Unfortunately I remembered no moment between us of special tenderness. On the other hand, generally speaking, tenderness permeated our friendship.

She shrugged.

When you were here before, of course. In April. When you came to tell me Tashi had run away from you. Even from your kisses.

Lisette

I had petit Pierre at home in my grandmother's bed. My grandmother, Béatrice, who spent her life fighting for the right of French women to vote. The low wooden bed that was built for the house in the century before the last and has never left it. The bed in which my mother was conceived and into which I myself was born. I ate well throughout my pregnancy, and went on long walks all over Paris nearly every day. My father and mother, after overcoming, to a remarkable degree, their normal outrage, racism and shock, showered me with advice and affection. It was recognized, in almost a formal way—*"Alors,* nothing can be done!" said my mother, shrugging at last after a bitter bout of tears—that I had inherited the genes of my mother's mother, who had had affairs, but no children, with Gypsies and Turks and the occasional Palestinian Jew, and, even worse, with penniless artists who could be found living in the literal garret of her tiny house and subsisting, again literally, on jars of jam and crusts of bread.

I had the most sought-after midwife in France—
my competent and funny aunt Marie-Thérèse, whose
radical idea it was that childbirth above all should
feel sexy. I listened to nothing but gospel music
during my pregnancy, a music quite new to me, and
to France, and "It's a High Way to Heaven"
(". . . nothing can walk up there, but the pure in
heart . . .") was playing on the stereo during the
birth; the warmth of the singers' voices a perfect
accompaniment to the lively fire in the fireplace. My
vulva oiled and massaged to keep my hips open and
my vagina fluid, I was orgasmic at the end. Petit
Pierre practically slid into the world at the height of
my amazement, smiling serenely even before he
opened his eyes.

My aunt placed him on my stomach the moment
she lifted him from between my legs, waiting to sever
the umbilical cord until he could breathe on his own;
and so, our heartbeats continued together as they
had while he was in my womb. Seeing his sleek tan
body and wet curly hair, I missed Adam. But, sighing
with completion, I soon sank into the pleasure of the
miracle I felt I and the universe alone had made.

He felt shut out, he said, when he was finally free
to come to us. Because he was not there.

But why? I asked. You knew when he was to be
born.

So did Evelyn, he said.

PART
SIX

Tashi-Evelyn

It is hot inside the courtroom. The ceiling fans, as they turn, sound like hoarse throats trying to clear themselves. The louvered windows are open fully to admit any semblance of breeze. I am dressed in cool white cotton from head to foot; Olivia shops for me in the tourist boutiques. Still, I feel perspiration beading at the center of my back, then slipping down in quicksilver rivulets to rest in an already sodden waistband.

It has been a morning spent listening to the words of those who saw me on my journey. The man who sold me the razors, a squat, rheumy-eyed fellow who admits he overcharged me because I was a foreigner. Although I spoke Olinka he could tell I was American by my dress, he said. Next, a woman who sold me an orange, as I was getting into the bus at Ombere station. She was old and toothless. Her rags obviously smelled, for both attorneys kept their distance as she sweated and drooled a bit there in the witness stand. It was a young woman, however, whose words appeared to nail me. She was thin and dark, with curious light pink, almost white lipsticked lips and painted nails. She explained, in English, with a word or two of Olinka sprinkled through it, that she was proprietress of the paper shop, hard by the square where one caught the bus. She remembered me because I had come into the shop looking for and then asking her to find for me sheets of thick white paper on which to print signs.

However, I'd changed my mind about wanting the white paper, she said, as soon as she brought some out to me.

No, she said I had said. White is not the culprit this time. Bring me out paper of the colors of our flag.

There was a sort of collective gasp in the courtroom when she said this. I felt even more eyes boring holes in the back of my neck. The judges surreptitiously scratched the natural kinky hair at the edges of their straight brush wigs.

And is this the paper, miss, that the defendant bought?

The prosecuting attorney stands before the young woman in the dock, the vivid red, yellow and blue paper held out in front of him.

There was a time the colors alone made me weep with pride. Now I look at them as dispassionately as if they were Crayolas in a child's coloring box.

Surprisingly, there are a few older people near the back of the courtroom who, on seeing the colors— for which they, as young bush revolutionaries, fought—stand, their hands over their hearts. (Of course I can not see them; I only hear, faintly, their movement. The creaking of joints, the shifting of feet. I don't even wonder about it at the time. Later Adam and Olivia will tell me. I think instead of the flag of my new home, America. I see, with my mind's eye, that red and blue and white flag. The meaning of whose colors is unknown to me. A flag a woman sewed.)

Reluctantly, I refocus on the young woman giving testimony. I think of the meaning of the word "testimony." Originally it named the custom of two men holding each other's testicles in a gesture of trust, later to metamorphose into the handshake. I imagine the woman's soft black hand cupping the young attorney's balls, her shell-pink nails deep in the tangles of his pubic hair. What are we doing in this sweltering courtroom, she is saying, brushing the ebony tips of her breasts against his smooth, hairless chest, it's actually a beautiful day outside. The attorney's face has that curious look of concentration sexually aroused men have; he . . . But I must pay attention, I think, rotating my head slowly on my neck; if I am not careful, I will have a torrid romance going, and miss, as Olivia says, my own trial.

The woman says I bought the paper and a Magic Marker pen and sat down immediately to draw my signs.

What signs did you see the defendant draw? asks the prosecutor.

Only one, says she.

Would you be good enough to tell the court how you happened to read this sign, and also what was written on it?

She showed it to me, said the young woman.

She showed it to you?

Yes. She said to me: You are a young woman and your life is still before you. I am an old woman and my life is already over. All I am good for now is alerting you to disaster.

Here the young woman paused, as if the emotion of this experience had momentarily pierced her. She raised a palely painted nail to the corner of her eye.

Of course I didn't understand, she said, as if to clear herself of any hint of collaboration.

Of course you did not, said the attorney. Please continue.

Well, said the young woman, she put down her bag, her suitcase, that is, and sat on it, over in a corner of the shop out of the way of traffic. Because it was rather early in the day, she was the only customer. She simply sat there and proceeded to make these signs.

And the one you saw? prompted the attorney.

The first one she drew, said the young woman. She held it out in front of her, gravely, and scanned it, then turned it toward me.

There was a silence.

I was surprised to read what it said. And of course I couldn't understand what it meant.

Right, said the attorney, waiting.

"If you lie to yourself about your own pain, you will be killed by those who will claim you enjoyed it." That is what the sign said; in big black letters. Said the young woman.

If you lie about your pain you will be killed, repeated the attorney.

To yourself, said the young woman. If you lie *to yourself.* This was obviously the part of the message that gripped her.

Yes, yes, said the attorney. And after she showed the sign to you, what did she do?

I believe she made several more. She explained to me that where she lived, in America, people make signs and buttons for everything they want to say, and no one ever arrests them for it. I warned her to be careful, said the young woman.

Why did you do that? asked the attorney, sharply. The young woman gave him a frightened look. Her voice dropped to a whisper as she replied. I don't know, she said.

But of course she knew. Everyone in the room knew. Half the people in prison in Olinka were there for expressing their discontent with the present government. An audible groan escaped me. The judges glared.

I had felt happy sitting on my red Chinese pigskin suitcase in the corner of the shop. Scribbling my big letters as if I were a child. It had occurred to me on the plane that never would I be able to write a book about my life, nor even a pamphlet, but that write *something* I could and would. And when the plane touched down all I saw were the billboards shouting out to the people that they must buy Fanta and Coca-Cola and Datsuns and Fords and chocolate and whiskey and sugar and more sugar and coffee and more coffee and tea and more tea. And I thought: Of course! This excrement is the reading matter of the masses. I am only one old and crazy woman, but I will fling myself against the billboards.

I will compete. And the next day, before leaving the city, I went bustling into the paper shop.

Why the colors of our flag? the attorney now asked.

But the young woman's blank expression was answer enough.

Why the colors of our flag indeed?

Red for the blood of the people spilled in resistance to the white supremacist regime. Yellow for the gold and minerals in which our land is still rich, even though the whites have carted mountains of it away. Blue for the sea that laps our shores, filled with riches and the wonders of the deep; blue also for the sky, symbol of our people's faith in the forces of the unseen and their optimism for the future.

There had been much debate about the colors of this flag; debate that included everyone. Then the colors were decided by the leaders and the flag sent off to Germany to be designed, mass produced and sold back to us.

I can feel my mind trying to kick off into an alternative flag story to replace the one that happened, in fact, to the people. But surprisingly, nothing happens. My head, like the rest of my body, remains solid in my chair. My refusing-to-leap imagination never makes it even as far as the open windows of the room. I have the uncanny feeling that, just at the end of my life, I am beginning to reinhabit completely the body I long ago left.

Olivia has crept up behind me as we all stand to be dismissed. She pushes a small paper bag into my hand. When I am in my cell again I open the bag and extract a small doll made of clay. It has been years since I saw another like it, quite by accident one morning in M'Lissa's hut. She found me playing with it, and boxed my ears, claiming the thing I held—a small figure playing with her genitals—was indecent. I was too young to ask why, therefore, she had it in her hut. A note from Olivia read: This is a replica. There are women potters here who make them. Can you imagine!

Frankly, I couldn't.

PART
SEVEN

Evelyn

The shrink The Old Man sent me to after his death was a middle-aged African-American woman named Raye. He had met her at a conference for psychologists in London when she was just starting out. They'd liked each other and kept in touch ever since. I resented her. Because she wasn't Mzee. Because she was black. Because she was a woman. Because she was whole. She radiated a calm, cheerful competence that irritated me.

It was to her, however, that I found myself speaking, one day, about Our Leader. Our Leader, like Nelson Mandela and Jomo Kenyatta and others before them, had been forced into exile and eventually captured and jailed by the white regime. Still, miraculously, by word of mouth and the occasional clandestinely made audiocassette, we were able to get his surprisingly frequent "Messages to the People." Unlike Nelson Mandela or Jomo Kenyatta, Our Leader never made it to freedom himself; he was assassinated on the eve of Independence as he left the high-security prison in which he'd been incarcerated, under heavy guard. It was believed, in fact, that the guards assassinated him, though this was never proved. His murderers, in any case, were never brought to justice, or even identified; and so, even as Olinkans celebrated what we thought was our freedom, there was already an internal backlash of hurt and rage that only swift justice administered to his killers might have assuaged, and the desperate need to show our remembrance and love of Our Leader in everything we did.

But you had already left Africa by then? said Raye, as I explained this to her.

Yes, I said. My body had left. My soul had not. I paused. It seemed impossible that anyone should ever understand. Especially not this smoothly dressed woman who walked with a spring in her step and whose brown skin, the color of cinnamon, was flawless.

There was a jaunty tone she sometimes took, at the most unlikely points. She used it now.

You can tell me, she said, with the look of a conspirator.

But I was stuck. Our Leader had died for us. For our independence. For our freedom. What could I possibly say about my insignificant life in the face of that reality? I could feel a boulder, twin to the one that suppressed the truth of Dura's murder, begin closing my throat. I felt a lie beginning to form. A lie that said the boulder was not a rock but rock candy. Then I remembered Mzee. You yourselves are your last hope, he'd said. Did I believe this, or not?

I cleared my throat, and began.

He was Jesus Christ to us, you know? I said, after the lengthy silence.

Raye looked at me expectantly.

If Jesus Christ has died for you, how can you find fault with anything else he did?

Some people fault him for claiming to die for them, said Raye. But we'll let that pass. Better to declare him perfect and be done, she added.

But what if he'd told you to do something that destroyed you? Something that was wrong?

Impossible, said Raye. He was perfect, remember.

But then she smiled impishly, and I saw the trap of such reasoning and also the joke in what she said. However, my jaws were too tight to smile.

I began again. Even from prison we received our instructions, I said. Good instructions. Sensible; correct. From Our Leader. That we must remember who we were. That we must fight the white oppressors without ceasing; without, even, the contemplation of ceasing; for they would surely still be around during our children's and our children's children's time. That we must take back our land. That we must reclaim the descendants of those of our people sold into slavery throughout the world (Our Leader was particularly strong on this issue, almost alone among African leaders); that we must return to the purity of our own culture and traditions. That we must not neglect our ancient customs.

There was another silence, as I played with the black plastic-looking elephant hair bracelets I wore on my wrist.

We thought him a god, really, I said finally, sighing. To have suffered so much . . . We knew they

117

had tortured him, we could even imagine how, based on the mutilated bodies sometimes returned to relatives from the prison. We knew he'd spent years in solitary and been driven nearly out of his mind. But he had not broken. Nor had he forgotten us.

In every hut, even when I was a little girl, there was a small picture of him wrapped in plastic and carefully hidden in a special place among the rafters. His eyes were laughing! Such wise, gay eyes. They seemed to speak. Whenever we received a message we took down the picture, and while going over the message and learning it by heart we would gaze at it. We loved him We believed everything he said. We thought he knew best . . . about everything.

The missionaries had made a big campaign against what they called the scarring of our faces with the Olinka tribal markings. But Our Leader had these same markings, and was obviously proud of them; and so it was difficult to hear the missionaries' objections, or to care about the missionaries themselves. Though we gave them our mumbled prayers and conversions, with which they seemed so easily, like mothers of docile children, satisfied.

Raye was leaning forward in her chair. As I spoke, I became aware I had covered both my cheeks with my fingers. I had also crossed my legs. I took my hands down and placed them in the folds of my dress. A light blue dress with aquamarine dots, it reminded me of the sea, and of tears.

As for the thing that was done to me . . . or *for* me, I said. And stopped. Because Raye had raised her eyebrows, quizzically.

The initiation . . .

Still she looked at me in the same questioning way.

The female initiation, I said. Into womanhood.

Oh? she said. But looked still as if she didn't understand.

Circumcision, I whispered.

Pardon? she said, in a normal tone of voice that seemed loud in the quiet room.

I felt as if I had handed her a small and precious pearl and she had promptly bitten into it and declared it a fake.

What exactly is this procedure? she asked, briskly.

I was reminded of a quality in African-American women that I did not like at all. A bluntness. A going to the heart of the matter even if it gave everyone concerned a heart attack. Rarely did black women in America exhibit the graceful subtlety of the African woman. Had slavery given them this? Suddenly a story involving Raye popped into my mind: I saw her clearly as she would have been in the nineteenth century, the eighteenth, the seventeenth, the six-teenth, the fifteenth . . . Her hands on her hips, her breasts thrust out. She is very black, as black as I am. "Listen, cracker," she is saying, "did you sell my child or not?" The "cracker" whines, "But listen, Louella, it was my child too!" The minute he turns his back, she picks up a huge boulder, exactly like the one that is in my throat, and . . . But I drag myself back from this scene.

Don't you have my file? I asked, annoyed. I was sure The Old Man sent it before he died. On the other hand, this was a question he'd never asked me.

I'd said "circumcision" to him and he'd seemed completely satisfied; as if he knew exactly what was implied. Now I wondered: had he understood?

I have your file, said Raye, tapping its bulging gray cover with a silver-painted nail and ignoring my attitude. I am ignorant about this practice, though, and would like to learn about it from you. She paused, glanced into the folder. For instance, something I've always wondered is whether the exact same thing is done to every woman. Or is there variation? Your sister . . . Dura's clitoris was excised, but was something else done too, that made it more likely that she would bleed to death?

Her tone was now clinical. It relaxed me. I breathed deeply and sought the necessary and familiar distance from myself. I did not get as far away as usual, however.

Always different, I would think, I said, exhaling breath, because women are all different. Yet always the same, because women's bodies are all the same. But this was not precisely true. In my reading I had discovered there were at least three forms of circumcision. Some cultures demanded excision of only the clitoris, others insisted on a thorough scraping away of the entire genital area. A sigh escaped me as I thought of explaining this.

A slight frown came between Raye's large, clear eyes.

I realize it is hard for you to talk about this, she said. Perhaps we shouldn't push.

But I am already pushing, and the boulder rolls off my tongue, completely crushing the old familiar faraway voice I'd always used to tell this tale, a voice that had hardly seemed connected to me.

It was only after I came to America, I said, that I even knew what was supposed to be down there.

Down there?

Yes. My own body was a mystery to me, as was the female body, beyond the function of the breasts, to almost everyone I knew. From prison Our Leader said we must keep ourselves clean and pure as we had been since time immemorial—by cutting out unclean parts of our bodies. Everyone knew that if a woman was not circumcised her unclean parts would grow so long they'd soon touch her thighs; she'd become masculine and arouse herself. No man could enter her because her own erection would be in his way.

You believed this?

Everyone believed it, even though no one had ever seen it. No one living in our village anyway. And yet the elders, particularly, acted as if everyone had witnessed this evil, and not nearly a long enough time ago.

But you knew this had not happened to you?

But perhaps it had, I said. Certainly to all my friends who'd been circumcised, my uncircumcised vagina was thought of as a monstrosity. They laughed at me. Jeered at me for having a tail. I think they meant my labia majora. After all, none of them had vaginal lips; none of them had a clitoris; they had no idea what these things looked like; to them I was bound to look odd. There were a few other girls who had not been circumcised. The girls who had been would sometimes actually run from us, as if we were demons. Laughing, though. Always laughing.

And yet it is from this time, before circumcision, that you remember pleasure?

When I was little I used to stroke myself, which was taboo. And then, when I was older, and before we married, Adam and I used to make love in the fields. Which was also taboo. Doing it in the fields, I mean. And because we practiced cunnilingus.

Did you experience orgasm?

Always.

And yet you willingly gave this up in order to . . . Raye was frowning in disbelief.

I completed the sentence for her: To be accepted as a real woman by the Olinka people; to stop the jeering. Otherwise I was a thing. Worse, because of my friendship with Adam's family and my special relationship to him, I was never trusted, considered a potential traitor, even. Besides, Our Leader, our Jesus Christ, said we must keep all our old ways and that no Olinka man—in this he echoed the great liberator Kenyatta—would even think of marrying a woman who was not circumcised.

But Adam was not Olinkan, said Raye, puzzled.

I sighed. The boulder was gone, but speech itself suddenly felt quite hopeless. I never thought of marrying Adam, I said, firmly, and watched the surprise in her eyes. I married him because he was loyal, gentle and familiar. Because he came for me. And because I found I could not fight with the wound tradition had given me. I could hardly walk.

But who . . . ? Raye began, even more perplexed.

At last I found a cool smile forming on my tense

face. I smiled at the young innocent, ignorant girl I'd been. The boulder now not only had rolled off my tongue but was rolling quite rapidly away from me toward the door. Like every Olinka maiden, I said, I was in love with the perfect lover who already had three wives. The perfect lover and father and brother who had been so cruelly taken from us, but whose laughing eyes we saw in the photograph he'd left us, and whose sweetly tempting voice we heard on cassette in the night. Poor Adam! He couldn't hold a candle to Our Leader, the real—to us—Jesus Christ.

Adam

The Olinkans spoke of "Our Leader" with exactly the fervor we wished them to speak of "Our Lord." There were always tales of his exploits drifting through the village, his "miracles" of ambush and derring-do against the whites. He seemed like Christ to the villagers except for one thing: his acceptance of violence as a means to the end of African oppression.

He was called "Our Leader" because the white regime made it a crime to say his name aloud. There were men walking about in every Olinka village whose backs bore the scars of their forgetfulness or defiance of this edict. And when these men spoke of "Our Leader," an especially harsh protectiveness and anger blazed in their eyes. In fact, it became increasingly frightening to try to talk to them about Christ at all. Our Christ. Our white, pacifist leader safely dead.

PART
EIGHT

PART
EIGHT

Lisette

When Pierre turned seventeen and had completed his studies at the *lycée,* nothing could prevent him from going to America to be nearer his father. He is thoughtful, curly-haired, golden. In France, people assume he is Algerian. I sent him to Harvard. Why not? As I tell my friends, since Pierre is my only expense, I can afford to be lavish with him. But it is more than that. Because he has grown up virtually without a father, I feel compelled to compensate.

When Evelyn learned of my pregnancy with little Pierre, as Adam and I and my parents used to call him, she flew into a rage that subsided into a years-long deterioration and rancorous depression. She tried to kill herself. She spoke of murdering their son. I felt badly for Adam. He had not intended to have a child with me. It was I who wanted a baby. I who did not want, except occasionally, a man. Perhaps I was simply swept along by the winds of change that were blowing over women's lives in France, thanks to women like my suffragist grandmother and writers like Simone de Beauvoir, whose book *The Second Sex* put the world I knew into a perspective I could more easily comprehend, if not control. Prior to reading her book I felt doomed to incomprehension regarding the universal subjugation of women. Doomed to ignorance, in spite of having listened, from babyhood, to the flaming speeches of Grandmother Béatrice, as she labored for the rights of French women. Doomed, even, to a kind of insanity that I believe the pampered oppressed always feel, and for which there seems to be no remedy except enlightenment regarding their plight, followed by active exercise of the insights of their awareness.

It was hard enough to have been forced to leave Algeria, our house and gardens and servants and friendships (with the servants) there. But the French were killing the Algerians, body and soul, and the Algerians grew sick of being treated worse than dogs. They fought back. There seemed to be a rising tide of blood across the land, and even clergymen like my father were not exempt. We left in tears, for we considered ourselves Algerians. French Algerians, of course. Members of the ruling class and race, *bien sûr*. The elite. And yet I, especially, felt native to the land, because I was. I was reborn there. Hot sun even now is the kind I prefer. I am never so happy as when enveloped by a scorching Parisian summer, when most true Parisians make sure to be someplace else. Someplace cooler. The ocean or the mountains.

There were places—restaurants, nightclubs, schools, neighborhoods—the Algerian natives could not go. The old colonial story. And yet the people were so beautiful, hospitable as Africans are always, especially our servants and playmates. The children taught me games, and they and their parents taught me Arabic.

There was no way I could understand what was happening, when they arrived for work with their eyes veiled, even hostile, and their faces swollen from grief. Some loved one would have been picked up by the French security forces in the night, grilled, imprisoned, tortured, killed.

Loving my nurse, my playmates and the servants, I naturally hated France. And then suddenly to have to "return" there, as the newspapers said of us. I protested to my parents that France was a place I'd never been; how, therefore, could I "return"? My parents, like most settler parents, had no answer. They were far from happy about the turn of events themselves. They'd left France in the first place because French society had no place for them; all prominent spots, my father joked, having been occupied; and though in Algeria my father suffered as a Christian minister surrounded by a world of Moslems, he felt he'd discovered and enlarged a niche for himself that was rewarding. He had more power in Algeria, and a more conspicuous place in society, than he ever could have had in France.

I liked to watch my father with petit Pierre, his namesake. They were physically much alike, short, thin-bodied and serious, rather slow and low-key among the coffee-crazed, perpetually cranky Parisians. I know that when my father looked at Pierre he saw the innocent, that is to say, apolitical, Algerian boys of his congregation whom he'd left behind to an uncertain fate, caught as they were between the French security forces, to whom all Arabs looked alike, and the Maquis, the NLA and the more militant Moslem fanatics, to whom Christian Arabs looked not at all like themselves: which is to say, like true Arabs. The young boys who had appeared deeply moved by the nonviolence preached by the Jesus Christ of my father's church. The Jesus they inevitably identified as a rebel Algerian, for not only did the Jesus Christ of the Christian religion look like an Algerian, but for a long time there was a tradition of Arab martyrdom in Algeria, of which they were well aware, as young "Arab terrorist" after young "Arab terrorist," sometimes boys no older than themselves, went up, barehanded or with stones and rusty swords, against the machine guns and hand grenades of the French.

Petit Pierre, appearing years later, after my parents had resettled completely into French life, and I had settled for the first time, became both our remembrance of our Algerian experience, which in Paris seemed suddenly never to have existed, and our solace. This became true even for my mother, who cared, to a much greater extent than either my father or I, what other people thought. She did not have her own mother's firm belief in her right to enjoy life as she pleased and in such company as she alone chose, but she had loved Algeria and the warmth of the people had impressed itself upon her. Her bourgeois French racism—"All Arabs steal; the women are no better than they should be; the children are born with a criminal streak; etc., etc.,

etc."—had been severely shaken by the suffering of her servants and friends.

She adored Pierre. When he left for America I thought her heart would break. She who saw him as the light of her waning existence, and the light of her memory of an earlier phase, in which he had had no part, but rather was like a belated sun in the evening of her life, illuminating some new truth she now knew, pointing backward with its rays. She who, since he could walk, had strolled hand in hand with him in every Paris square. Protectively wary at first of the covert glances of strangers; then boldly in solidarity with petit Pierre; then lost, happily, in the grandmotherly joy of his golden hand in hers.

Evelyn

I told Raye about my lifelong tendency to escape from reality into the realm of fantasy and storytelling.

Without this habit, I said, it would be impossible for me to guess anything out of the ordinary had happened to me.

What do you mean? she asked.

I mean, if I find myself way off into an improbable tale, imagining it or telling it, then I can guess something horrible has happened to me and that I can't bear to think about it. Wait a minute, I said, considering it for the first time, do you think this is how storytelling came into being? That the story is only the mask for the truth?

She looked doubtful.

I grew to trust Raye. One day when I went in to see her I found her with her cheeks puffed out like a squirrel. Her skin was ashen and she looked awful.

What's the matter? I asked.

She grimaced. Gum mutilation, she said, with her lips pursed.

Later, when she could speak more clearly, she told me how it had bothered her that the kind of pain I must have endured during circumcision was a pain she could hardly imagine; and so, having been told by her dentist that she had several pockets of gum disease, in an otherwise healthy mouth, she'd had her gums turned down like socks around her teeth, their edges clipped and insides scraped, and then sewed up again, tight, around the roots of her teeth.

I could not prevent an involuntary shudder of disgust.

But of course I had anesthesia, she said, still speaking as if her gums were stitched. And of course in a few days I'll be better than before.

But you are obviously in pain now, I said.

Yes, she admitted. And it is nearly impossible for me to bear it, and also talk. Not surprisingly, making love to anyone at all is the furthest thing from my mind. She laughed. And this is only in my mouth!

You shouldn't have done it, I said coldly. It was stupid of you.

But she only chuckled, grimacing painfully as she did so. Don't be mad because my choosing this kind of pain seems such a puny effort, she said. In America it's the best I can do. Besides, it gives me a faint idea. *And* it was something I needed to do anyway.

I was angry because I was touched. I realized that though Raye had left Africa hundreds of years before in the persons of her ancestors and studied at the

133

best of the white man's schools, she was intuitively practicing an ageless magic, the foundation of which was the ritualization, or the acting out, of empathy. How theatre was born? My psychologist was a witch, not the warty kind American children imitate on Halloween, but a spiritual descendant of the ancient healers who taught our witch doctors and were famous for their compassionate skill. Suddenly, in that guise, Raye became someone I felt I knew; someone with whom I could bond.

In my heart I thanked Mzee for her, for I believed she would be plucky enough to accompany me where he could not. And that she would.

Pierre

It was a rainy December afternoon and we sat by the fire, reading. My mother sat; I lounged on the sofa across from her. Earlier that morning she had permitted me to sleep late, missing school, and had brought her gifts to me and spread them across the foot of my bed. Each year since my birth she'd knitted me a sweater. Each year I watched the piece of knitting grow between her flashing needles; each year I was charmed by the result. This year, as every year, she'd outdone herself. The new sweater wrapped me in gold and chocolate; near the center of my chest, just above my heart, there was a petroglyphic spirit head in a rich, mossy green.

I was reading a book by Langston Hughes, the laughing spellbinder whose sadness almost hid itself in the insouciance of his prose. I had already devoured several novels by James Baldwin, the guerrilla homosexual genius whom I had met once when he came to speak at our school, and two volumes of

essays by Richard Wright, the tortured assimilation-
ist and great lover of France. These men, "uncles"
from my father's side, would be my guides on my
American journey. I glanced over at my mother,
expecting to find her still reading, or staring thoughtfully into the fire, but finding instead that her warm
brown eyes were fixed on me.

I was just thinking, she said. It has been sixteen
years since you were born. I can't believe it.

That long? I said, smiling at her.

Her brown hair was dusted with more gray than
I'd noticed before, and her face seemed thinner than
usual, and more pale. I sighed with the contentment
of the spoiled only child, and pondered my good
fortune. I felt the greatest possible security with my
mother. As she often said, our hearts had beat as one
since before my birth. No matter who else was *not* in
my life, there was always my mother: reading, knitting, preparing for her classes at the *lycée*. It was true
that I was beginning to feel ready to separate from
her, but gently, as a fruit drops from the tree. One
more year of school, of Paris, and I would be gone.

If you go to America, she said—as if I might not
after all our years of planning—and spend time with
your father, there's something you should know.

What? I asked.

Something minor, perhaps. But he won't remember it. And I do.

How mysterious, I said.

Not so mysterious! she said. It's just that I've
realized with your father that men refuse to remember things that don't happen to them.

Full of the passionate words of Baldwin, Hughes

and Wright, which rang in my heart as if already inscribed there, I leaned forward to protest. My mother put out her hand and covered my lips.

For as long as I could remember, my father came to see me and my mother once in fall and once in spring; for two weeks each visit. He never came on my birthday, because coming at that time seriously distressed his wife. Each time he came he showed me photographs of his other son, Benny, and at least one photograph of his wife, Evelyn, or, as he sometimes called her, Tashi. Benny was nearly three years older than me, with bronze satiny skin and a sweet, tentative smile. Whenever I saw a new photo of him I wondered if he'd like me. If we could ever be friends. Once, my father told me that Benny wasn't as "quick" as I. This pleased me enormously, though I hadn't the words to ask him what a lack of "quickness" like mine might mean.

My mother began to tell me the story of how she met my father, years ago in Africa. I'd heard it before. I nodded complacently as she talked about the hours she spent with my father in Old Torabe's hut, as the old man waited for death. But I soon realized my mother was adding a more adult twist than usual to the tale.

You have to understand, she said, there was a reason why Old Torabe lived alone, way outside the village, and why none of the villagers came to care for him. Your father certainly didn't enjoy caring for him, either; your grandfather Samuel assigned Torabe to him.

My mother uncrossed her legs, pressed her palms against the arms of her chair in order to stretch her back and glanced from me to the fire, which would soon need another log.

In his youth Torabe had had many wives. A few of them died. In childbirth. From infection. One died from snakebite. In any event—and I learned this from Adam, who liked to recount the old man's, as he called them, "negative blessings"—at last Torabe married a young woman who ran away from him, and could not be brought back. He'd been notorious for tracking and bringing back his runaway wives before. This one drowned herself, in water that didn't even reach her knees, rather than return.

She'd gone to her parents and asked them how they expected her to endure the torture: he had cut her open with a hunting knife on their wedding night, and gave her no opportunity to heal. She hated him. Her parents had no answer for her. Her father instructed her mother to convince her of her duty. Because she was Torabe's wife, her place was with him, her mother told her. The young woman explained that she bled. Her mother told her it would stop: that when she herself was cut open she bled for a year. She had also cried and run away. Never had she gotten beyond the territory of men who returned her to her tribe. She had given up, and endured. Now her mother stood in the shadow of the girl's father, a man she despised, waiting for death, but, in the meantime, longing for grandchildren, which she hoped this errant daughter would provide. There is nothing in the world to kiss but small children, said the mother, turning away from her daughter's tears.

Torabe was thrown out of the village because he lost control of his wife, a very evil thing to do in that society because it threatened the fabric of the web of life. At least the web of life as the villagers knew it. He died deserted, filthy and in tatters. The girl's family too was ordered out of the village, and the girl herself was dragged from the river and left to rot, her body food for vultures and rodents.

Now, said my mother, rising to place a log on the fire, your father always mentions the fact that he and I had "lively" conversation there in Torabe's hut, as he reluctantly washed the old man, but he never remembers what our conversation was about.

It was, said my mother, about a young woman in Algeria who worked for us, and who nearly suffered the same fate as Torabe's wife. It was about how, at last, I recognized the connection between mutilation and enslavement that is at the root of the domination of women in the world. Her name was Ayisha, and she ran to us one night screaming from the sight of the variety of small, sharp instruments her anxious mother had arranged underneath a napkin on a low seating cushion that rested beside the bridal bed.

My mother suddenly shuddered, as though watching a frightful scene. It's in all the movies that terrorize women, she said, only masked. The man who breaks in. The man with the knife. Well, she said, he has already come. She sighed. But those of us whose chastity belt was made of leather, or of silk and diamonds, or of fear and not of our own flesh . . . we worry. We are the perfect audience, mesmerized by our unconscious knowledge of what men, with the collaboration of our mothers, do to us.

After a long pause she said: This episode with Ayisha, who was returned to her family, who beat her for running away—and actually we never knew what became of her—is at the root of my refusal to marry; even though in France there are no instruments of torture beside the bed.

And the Marquis de Sade? I asked.

Thankfully only one man, she said, and thankfully not in this century. She laughed. And thankfully not beside *my* bed.

Perhaps, I said. But surely his cruelty to women is lodged in the collective consciousness of the French? Like the zest of Rabelais, the wit of Molière?

Perhaps, she murmured, and seemed to lose herself gazing into the fire.

PART NINE

Evelyn

I felt no compunction about opening letters that came from Lisette to Adam, letters which sometimes contained copies of letters she'd received from her uncle Mzee touching on my case; or even, sometimes, copies of letters from Adam himself; she seemed often to need to jog his memory about something or other. There was an occasional copied page of her diary in which she appeared contented, and self-possessed: autonomous in a way I could not imagine for myself. She also had the nerve occasionally to address a letter to me. These always sounded as if she were feeling her way through fog. I trampled them. I routinely, and leisurely, read those from her which Adam left lying open at the back of his bottom desk drawer, the key to which I had long since duplicated. It was from one of her letters that I learned their son, Pierre, was coming to America.

Informing me he was going to a gathering of progressive *religieux,* Adam flew to Boston to meet

143

him and was gone a week, helping Pierre settle into the life of Cambridge and Harvard. The boy was still far away, the breadth of the continent, so I did not worry. He remained in Cambridge for three years.

It was from her letters that I learned of Lisette's illness. Diagnosed first as stress brought on by her political activity: she was active in the movement against French nuclear power plants, which, she wrote, dotted like dangerous *pustules* the once pristine countryside; later diagnosed as an ulcer. Then as a hernia. Then, finally, as stomach cancer. She petitioned Adam to permit Pierre to live with him and to attend Berkeley after her death. This Adam apparently agreed to do; I refused to let him bring up the subject with me.

It was during a period when I could not eat and was emaciated as a scarecrow; my clothes hung on me, and I wore nothing that wasn't black. The week before, someone introduced to me by Adam said, with a snigger: "Ah, Adam and *Eve*lyn. How cute!" And I slapped him.

I felt the violence rising in me with every encounter with the world outside my home. Even inside it I frequently and with little cause, *no* cause, boxed Benny's ears. If I made him squeal and cringe and look at me with eyes gone grave with love and incomprehension, I fancied I felt relief.

I was watching the street when the taxi came. A boxy, bright yellow, child's cartoon of a taxi. The kind of taxi the world expects all American taxis to be. I glimpsed Pierre's curly head before he got out, as he leaned forward to pay the driver. He was skinny and short, as if still a child. I watched the two

of them, chatting like old friends, go around to the
boot to take out his bags.

Still chatting, they did not notice the dark spectre
floating near them: first to the door, then to the
porch, then to the steps, alighting to stoop beside a
large pile of stones I had begun to collect the very
day I learned of Pierre's birth. Large oblong stones
from the roadside; heavy flat stones from the river-
bank; sharp jagged shale stones from the fields.

As Pierre thanked the driver and turned toward
the house, he saw me, and smiled. A large jagged
stone, gray as grief, struck him just above the teeth.
Blood spurted from his nose. I began to throw the
stones as if, like Kali, I had a dozen arms, or as if my
arms were a multiple catapult or a windmill. Stones
rained upon him and upon the cab, which had
started to pull off but screeched to a stop as the
driver realized Pierre was under attack and sinking
to one knee. I did not let up, but floated nearer,
cradling an armful of stones. Pierre began to speak in
a gibberish of French, which infuriated me. I
dropped the stones in order to close my ears with the
palms of my hands. During this interlude, the cabbie
ran up to Pierre, grabbed him under the arms and
dragged him out of sight.

I began to laugh, as the taxi disappeared down the
street. In their cowardly haste they'd forgotten
Pierre's luggage. The brown suitcases sat, importu-
nate and irrevocable, where he'd dropped them;
more heavy baggage for me to lift and somehow
carry. I would not. I dove forward, flapping my arms
and shrieking hoarsely like a crow, to kick them into
the street.

PART
TEN

PART
TEN

Evelyn

The bus ride from Ombere station was long. The roads bumpy. The dust everywhere. Each twenty-five kilometers or so we stopped to use roadside facilities. These were not at all like those in America but were entirely makeshift. Smelly holes in the earth on either side of which some forward-thinking person had nailed a board. On these boards, inevitably splashed with urine, one placed one's feet.

A week ago I would not have expected M'Lissa to still be alive. But yes, according to a year-old *Newsweek* I perused in the waiting room of the Waverly, she was not only alive but a national monument. She had been honored by the Olinka government for her role during the wars of liberation, when she'd acted as a nurse as devoted to her charges as Florence Nightingale, and for her unfailing adherence to the ancient customs and traditions of the Olinka state. No mention was made of how

149

she fulfilled this obligation. She had been decorated, "knighted," the magazine said; swooped up from her obscure hut, where she lay dying on a filthy straw mat, and brought to a spacious cottage on the outskirts of a nearby town, where she would be within easy commute to a hospital, should the need arise.

After being brought out of her dark hut and into the sunlight of her new home—with running water and an indoor toilet, both miracles to the lucky M'Lissa—a remarkable change had occurred. M'Lissa had stopped showing any signs of death, stopped aging, and had begun to actually blossom. "Youthen," as the article said. A local nurse, a geriatrics specialist, ministered to her; a cook and a gardener rounded out her staff. M'Lissa, who had not walked in over a year, began again to walk, leaning on a cane the president himself had given her, and enjoyed tottering about in her garden. She loved to eat, and kept her cook on his toes preparing the special dishes of lamb curry, raisin rice and chocolate mousse she particularly liked. She had a mango tree; indeed, the photograph showed her sitting beneath it; she sat there happily, day after day, when the crop came on, stuffing herself.

In the photograph M'Lissa smiled broadly, new teeth glistening; even her hair had grown back and was a white halo around her deep brown head.

There was something sinister, though, about her aspect; but perhaps I was the only one likely to see it. Though her mouth was smiling, as were her sunken cheeks and her long nose, her wrinkled forehead and her scrawny neck, her beady eyes were not. Looking into them, suddenly chilled, I realized they never had.

How had I entrusted my body to this madwoman?

Tashi-Evelyn

A flag flew above her house, the red, yellow and blue vivid against the pale noonday periwinkle sky. I was not her only visitor; there were cars parked in the postage-stamp parking lot, neatly screened from the house by a rose-colored bougainvillea, and a tour bus was halted by the road. The passengers were not permitted to disembark, but were busy taking photographs of the cottage from the windows of the bus. I left my rental car out of view of the house, and when I walked up the red steps to the porch and looked back, I felt surprise that it had disappeared. Not seeing the vehicle of my arrival seemed right, however, after a moment's reflection, for I experienced all the more a feeling I'd begun to have in the openness of the countryside: that I had flown direct, as if I were a bird, from my house to hers, and that this had been accomplished with the directness of thought: a magical journey.

I was met on the porch by a young woman who

had not been mentioned in the *Newsweek* article: slender, with smooth dark skin and shining eyes, as lovely as a freshly cut flower. I explained I'd known M'Lissa all my life; that she had in fact delivered me into the world, having been a great friend of my mother and in fact mother of the entire village. I explained I had come from America, where I now lived, even though Olinka by birth, and that I hoped to spend time with M'Lissa, perhaps after her other guests had gone.

What is your name? she asked softly.

Tell her it is Tashi, Catherine's, no, *Nafa's* daughter, who went to America with the son of the missionary.

She turned. Out of habit I glanced down at her feet. As she moved away, I saw she had the sliding gait of the "proper" Olinka maiden.

Within minutes all of M'Lissa's guests poured out of the house, as if scattered by her cane. They scrutinized me as they passed. Perhaps they thought me an important dignitary. As their car motors were turning over, shattering the quiet, the young woman returned.

You may go in, she said, with a smile.

What is *your* name? I asked her.

Martha, she replied.

And your other name?

Mbati, she said, her eyes twinkling.

Mbati, I said, why do the people come here?

The question surprised her. Mother Lissa is a national monument, she said. Recognized as a heroine by every faction of the government, including the

153

National Liberation Front. She's famous, she said, shrugging her shoulders and looking at me as if puzzled I didn't know.

I do know that, I said. I read *Newsweek*.

Ah, *Newsweek,* she said.

But what do they talk about with her?

About their daughters. About the old ways. About tradition. She paused. It is mostly women who come. You may have noticed this by the people who just left. Women of a certain age. Women with daughters. Frightened women, often. She reassures them.

Oh? I said.

Yes. She knows so much and says such bizarre things. Why, do you know, Mama Lissa claims there was a time when women did not have periods! Oh, she says, there may have been a single drop of blood, but only one! She says this was before woman's capture.

I couldn't help laughing, as Mbati was doing.

She just sits and talks; holds court. It hardly matters what she says. She is probably a hundred; everyone wants to have been in her presence before she dies. So much, as you know, has fallen apart here: independence is killing us as surely as colonialism did. But then, she added, sighing, that is because it isn't really independence.

Mbati takes my hand and pulls me slowly forward, still speaking quietly. She is a link with the past for us; especially for us women, she says. She is the only woman honored in this way by the government; she is an ikon.

How is it possible, I think, as Mbati leads me into M'Lissa's sparkling hallway and pushes me into

M'Lissa's room and toward a snow white bed, that my mother has lived and died; Mzee has lived and died; the Frenchwoman Lisette has lived and died; I myself have lived and died—in and out of the Waverly, in and out of my mind—many times. World wars have been fought and lost; for every war is against the world and every war against the world is lost. But look, here lies M'Lissa, propped up like a queen in her snowy bed, the open window beside it looking out into a fragrant garden, and in the distance, above the garden, there is a blue mountain. She is radiant, and her forehead, nose, lips, teeth, cheeks smile at me. I bend to kiss the top of her head, her white hair a resistant brush against my lips. I take her hand, which has the feel of feathers, and stand a moment looking down at her. Her whole body is smiling her welcome; except for her eyes. They are wary and alert. I had thought when people aged, their eyes went bad. But no, she sees me clearly. Hers is an x-ray gaze. But then, so is mine, now. What is that shadow, there in the depths? Is it apprehension? Is it fear?

PART
ELEVEN

PART
ELEVEN

Evelyn

Mbati is taking the stand. She wears no makeup or jewelry and her hair is short and natural. There is a simplicity about her that dignifies the whole room. When she speaks the warm quietness of her personality soothes the court, even if the hoarse cry of the ceiling fans becomes more grating than ever. She is the daughter I should have had. Perhaps could have had, had I not aborted her out of fear.

I float up to the stand and hover, a large dragonfly, in front of her. Reaching out, I take her smooth hand in mine. Her eyes widen: with wonder; with delight. Come, I say to her, smiling, I am your mother. If you take my hand before all of these people, all of these judges, all of these policemen and warders and rubbernecks in the audience, you will discover that the two of us can fly. Really? she asks, placing her other hand also in mine. I tug gently and she leaves her seat and floats beside me over the railing of the witness stand, over the attorneys' tables, over the heads of the packed courtroom . . . out the door and into the sky. We are lighter than air, lighter than thistle. Mother and daughter heading for the sun.

No, I suspected nothing, she is saying, when I float back into myself, sitting on the hard chair next to my attorney.

They were old friends. Mother Lissa knew her. She was happy to see her. In fact, I'd never seen her so excited. They needed to talk. Time alone. Mother Lissa insisted.

And so you left your post. Left *Mother* Lissa's bedside. Even left the house, the attorney says accusingly.

My daughter drops her head. But quickly looks up again. There is that healthy, impish twinkle in her eyes she sometimes gets.

She turns her face to the judges. Your Honors, she says, firmly, I left the vicinity.

They all ignore this spark of life. This simple authenticity. This beauty.

Objection, says the other attorney. (I can no longer really tell them apart; the only way I recognize which attorney is mine is by noticing which of them sits next to me, and by the way he smells: his cologne is a scent popular in America.) The defendant's fiendish behavior is not something which, in advance, the witness could have known.

Did you suspect anything? prods the attorney.

The child looks pained. I feel sorry for her. How could they imagine any of this is her fault? It was I who shooed Mbati from her post; I who told M'Lissa: Mama Lissa, give the girl a break. Your other daughter has come from America just to look after you! Since this coming back to care for the elderly was such a strong characteristic of the ancient traditions, how could she refuse?

Oh, M'Lissa had said, it is too much happiness. Too much! To see the daughter of Nafa, here, right beside my bed. Oh, surely I shall die of it!

I thought it an odd thing to say.

How did the defendant appear to you? the prosecuting attorney asks.

There is a long pause. Motherly, Mbati replies.

The young man is surprised. What, his look implies, this demon, *motherly!*

Yes, Mbati continues in a definite voice. I lost my own mother when I was an infant, and yet never believed she died. When Mrs. Johnson showed up at the door—

Childhood memories are quite irrelevant to this court, says the attorney, cutting her off. Though surely the humane response would have been to let her finish; even if one felt quite unable to ask the question: How did your mother die? It is a taboo question, in Olinka. One never asked for fear of the answer.

Mbati subsides into silence, but looks me in the face and holds my gaze. I see she has not condemned me.

Evelyn

My heart goes out to Adam, physically stout, emotionally frail; perspiration beading on his upper lip. It is hard to believe this grayhaired and gray-bearded old man is my husband, and has been my dearest friend for over fifty years. And was my lover.

He looks condemned, simply to be present in the jammed court. He stares up disconsolately at the recently oiled, slowly whirring ceiling fans, or out the open windows, awaiting the thrust and parry of the attorneys' questions.

I remember when his body was slender and firm, and how I used to kiss from nipple to nipple across the smooth expanse of his beautiful chest.

He is saying I am a tortured woman. Someone whose whole life was destroyed by the enactment of a ritual upon my body which I had not been equipped to understand.

As soon as he utters the word "ritual" there is a furor in the court. Male voices, and female voices, calling for Adam's silence. Shut up, shut up, you disgraceful American! the voices cry. This is our business you would put into the streets! We cannot publicly discuss this taboo.

Adam looks weary. About to weep.

Mother Lissa was a monument! the voices hiss. Your wife has murdered a monument. The Grandmother of the race!

I feel the furies, the shrieking voices, wrap their coils around my neck. But rather than allowing myself to choke, I become a part of the shrieking and rise from around my own neck exactly as if I were wind. I blow and blow about the court, building toward explosion.

The judges call for order, over and over. The other furies and I subside. At last order is restored.

I am thinking of how I never met Lisette. How she tried to know me. Tried to visit me. Wrote me letters. Tried to interest me in French cooking—sent me cookbooks and recipes. Sent me clippings about wild mushrooms and where to look for them. (None of this is helpful, I used to mutter to myself, gazing into the mirror and sticking out my tongue.) Sent me her son. And how I refused her. How I thought she knew me too well.

And then suddenly, after a long, painful struggle, she died. Leaving Pierre her eyes—for his eyes are not Adam's—and it was those knowing eyes, with their appraising look, that, from as far away as an undergraduate dormitory at Harvard, saw into me. Even into my dreams.

Chère Madame Johnson, he wrote. I hope you will not tear up this letter before you read it. (At that point I of course tore it in half, then held the pieces

163

together to continue reading.) All my life I have heard about the tower that frightens you in your dreams. This tower question obsessed my mother since the day she heard of it, and she read many books trying to figure out what it could mean. It was an effort I shared, from the time I was a small boy. Always in the back of my mind has hovered this compelling nightmare of yours, told only once to my mother by my father, but told so vividly our house was never quite free of it.

For as we both understood it, this nightmare, this *cauchemar* of yours, of being held captive in a dark tower, was what kept my father away from me.

Madame, I now know what the tower is, though not, perhaps, what it means.

As you know, I am now in Berkeley, which is not so far, after all, from your house.

Will you not throw stones?

Shall we meet?

Pierre Johnson

Adam

They do not want to hear what their children suffer. They've made the telling of the suffering itself taboo. Like visible signs of menstruation. Signs of woman's mental power. Signs of the weakness and uncertainty of men. When they say the word "taboo" I try to catch their eye. Are they saying something is "sacred" and therefore not to be publicly examined for fear of disturbing the mystery; or are they saying it is so profane it must not be exposed, for fear of corrupting the young? Or are they saying simply that they can not and will not be bothered to listen to what is said about an accepted tradition of which they are a part, that has gone on, as far as they know, forever?

These are the kinds of questions my father taught me to ask, alas. Adam, he would say, What is the fundamental question one must ask of the world? I would think of and posit many things, but the answer was always the same: *Why is the child crying?* There had been a crying child even in Old Torabe,

165

whose filth and age and illness so disgusted me. Before he died, I saw it. He had not loved the majority of his wives; in fact, he didn't even hate them; he thought of them as servants in the most disposable sense. He barely remembered their names. But the young woman who ran away, the wife who drowned herself, he had at least thought he loved. Unfortunately, for him, "love" and frequent, forceful sex were one. And so he lay, finally, wounded and wet with his own tears, lamenting his life but knowing no other. Women are indestructible down there, you know, he'd said to me, lewdly, more than once, his eyes alight with remembered lechery and violence. They are like leather: the more you chew it, the softer it gets.

If every man in this courtroom had had his penis removed, what then? Would they understand better that that condition is similar to that of all the women in this room? That, even as we sit here, the women are suffering from the unnatural constrictions of flesh their bodies have been whittled and refashioned into? Not just Evelyn. But also the young woman from the paper shop; the old woman who sells oranges. The bourgeois women in their elegant robes, fanning themselves and powdering their noses against the humidity. The poor women packed tight against the back doors. The beautiful, daughterly woman, Mbati.

How wearying to think nobody in this courtroom has ever listened to them. I see each one of them as the little child my father was always so concerned about, screaming her terror eternally into her own ear.

We are aware, says the prosecutor, that Mrs.
Johnson, though Olinkan, has lived in America for
many, many years, and that American life is, for the
black person, itself a torture.

I stare at him blankly.

Is it not true, Mr. Johnson, that in the United
States, with its stressful whites, your wife is often
committed to an insane asylum?

My wife is *hurt,* I say. *Wounded. Broken.* Not mad.

Evelyn laughs. Flinging her head back in deliber-
ate challenge. The laugh is short. Sharp. The bark of
a dog. Beyond hurt. Unquestionably mad. Oddly
free.

Evelyn-Tashi

They would all take America away from me if they could. But I won't let them. If I have to, I'll stop them in their tracks. Just as I stopped Amy. How do you stop someone in their tracks? By not believing them.

Adam

Woman after woman comes to me to complain that her husband, man, lover, is or was unfaithful to her, says Tashi's new doctor, Raye, when we have a consultation. The result, nine times out of ten, is frigidity in the woman. Psychological circumcision? she asks, pensively.

I tell her I do not know. It had never occurred to me to think of Tashi's suffering as being on a continuum of pain. I had thought of what was done to her as something singular, absolute.

PART
TWELVE

Tashi-Evelyn

"The God Amma, it appeared, took a lump of clay, squeezed it in his hand and flung it from him, as he had done with the stars. The clay spread and fell on the north, which is the top, and from there stretched out to the south, which is the bottom, of the world, although the whole movement was horizontal. The earth lies flat, but the north is at the top. It extends east and west with separate members like a foetus in the womb. It is a body, that is to say, a thing with members branching out from a central mass. This body, lying flat, face upwards, in a line from north to south, is feminine. Its sexual organ is an anthill, and its clitoris a termite hill. Amma, being lonely and desirous of intercourse with this creature, approached it. That was the occasion of the first breach of the order of the universe. . . .

"At God's approach the termite hill rose up, barring the passage and displaying its masculinity. It was as strong as the organ of the stranger, and intercourse could not take place. But God is all-

173

powerful. He cut down the termite hill, and had intercourse with the excised earth. But the original incident was destined to affect the course of things forever. . . ."

As Pierre reads I study his face seeking signs of Adam, signs of Lisette. He seems a completely blended person and, as such, new. In him "black" has disappeared; so has "white." His eyes are a dark, lightfilled brown; his forehead is high and tan; his nose broad, a little flat. He has told me he likes men as well as he likes women, which seems only natural, he says, since he is the offspring of two sexes as well as of two races. No one is surprised he is biracial; why should they be surprised he is bisexual? This is an explanation I have never heard and cannot entirely grasp; it seems too logical for my brain. His brother sits across from him as he reads, sunk in admiration. They have stolen many hours to be together, roaming the Berkeley campus and the city's streets, happy to have found each in the other his own best friend.

Now he stops reading, suddenly, and looks at me. This is from a book by a French anthropologist, Marcel Griaule, he says, turning it so I can see its orange cover and read its title, *Conversations with Ogotemmêli*. I am under the influence of a new, mild and quite pleasant drug. It is as if I've smoked marijuana. I have not grasped the meaning of the passage, which Pierre has read to me so earnestly; nor do I completely comprehend how it is he is sitting in my living room reading to me from this strange book. Have I stopped hating him? I gaze at Benny, who looks so happy, and then down into my lap. My eyes sting the way they do when I'm drugged; closing them brings relief. Pierre is reading as if I am listening: "God had further intercourse with his earth-wife, and this time without mishaps of any kind, the excision of the offending member having removed the cause of the former disorder." I feel him stop, rustle the pages, and look over at me. I raise my eyes and attempt a bright look in his direction. I am awake, I say. Indeed, I am listening. However, as he resumes reading, the words, on touching my ear, bounce back into his mouth, as if they're made of India rubber. This is a distracting sight, and I look at Benny to see if he has noticed it. He hasn't. He sits enraptured, his notepad on his lap. Who taught him to write, I ask myself, if he can never remember anything?

"The spirit drew two outlines on the ground, one on top of the other, one male and the other female. The man stretched himself out on these two shadows of himself, and took both of them for his own. The same thing was done for the woman. Thus it came about that each human being from the first was endowed with two souls of different sex, or rather with two principles corresponding to two distinct persons. In the man the female soul was located in the prepuce; in the woman the male soul was in the clitoris."

Here I looked up. Pierre continued: "Man's life was not capable of supporting both beings: each person would have to merge himself in the sex for which he appeared to be best fitted." So, said Pierre, closing the book but keeping his finger between its pages, the man is circumcised to rid him of his femininity; the woman is excised to rid her of her masculinity. In other words, he said, leaning forward in his chair, a very long time ago, men found it necessary to permanently lock people in the category of their obvious sex, even while recognizing sexual duality as a given of nature.

How long ago was this? I ask, my focus somewhat blurred.

Pierre shrugged, and I fancied I saw his mother's body in the fluid ripple of his shoulders.

Even Cleopatra was circumcised, he says. Nefertiti, also. But some people think the people in this book, the Dogon, are from a civilization even older than theirs, and that this civilization spread northward, from central Africa *up* toward ancient Egypt and the Mediterranean. He paused, musing. My mother used to say genital mutilation, which predates all the major religions, was a kind of footbinding.

After he leaves the house to accompany Benny to a basketball game, I am left with the book, whose pages he has thoughtfully marked, and with the puzzle of his last comment. Suddenly I see Lisette very clearly. She is sitting by a window in front of which there is a desk. She is thinking of me as she looks into a thick brown book in front of her, and her white brow is puckered in a frown. She is gazing at a drawing of a tiny, putrid, Chinese woman's foot, and reading the notation that says the rotten smell was an aphrodisiac for the man, who liked to hold both small feet helpless in his large hand, raising them to his nose as he prepared to ravish the woman, who could not run away. This immobility most satisfying to his lust. The pain of her hobbling attempts to escape pure incentive to relish the chase. His mother has been conjured by the odd, unAmerican movement of Pierre's shoulders, as much as by his words. Why, I wonder, do we assume people who think deeply about us ever die?

As I open the book, my eye falls on a passage Pierre had not read: "The man then had intercourse with the woman, who later bore the first two children of a series of eight, who were to become the ancestors of the Dogon people. In the moment of birth the pain of parturition was concentrated in the woman's clitoris, which was excised by an invisible hand, detached itself and left her, and was changed into the form of a scorpion. The pouch and the sting symbolized the organ: the venom was the water and the blood of the pain."

I read the passage over again, my eye always stopped by the words "an invisible hand." Even so long ago God deserted woman, I thought, staying by her just long enough to illustrate to man the cutting to be done. And what if pain wasn't what she felt at the moment of parturition? After all, pain was what *I* felt, having given birth, and I did not have a clitoris for it to be concentrated in.

I read further: "The dual soul is a danger; a man should be male, and a woman female. Circumcision and excision are . . . the remedy."

But who could bear to think of this for long? I closed the book, wandered unsteadily across the room, flopped heavily onto the couch, and lost myself in a rerun of "HeeHaw" on TV.

Adam

It saddens me that Pierre has never married, and that he seems content to pursue his career as an anthropologist and to spend much of the time he has for himself with Benny. This petit (for a man) curly-haired, teak-colored person is my son! I am as astonished as he approaches middle age as I was when he was two. Though his voice is deep, deeper than mine, a person of color's voice, it still seems at times, because of his accent, the voice of a stranger. I see his mother in him. Lisette, who took so long to die, bravely determined to hold on to her dignity, her self, to the end; her thick, fierce French neck wasting away as she struggled. Only to beg, finally, for morphine and more and more morphine. Seeing her in Pierre makes the memory of my last visits with her bearable, and reactivates happier thoughts of our earlier days.

Pierre laughs at my concern, gracefully refraining from observing aloud that my own marriage has been hellacious.

I am married to my work, he says.

But your work does not produce children, I counter.

He smiles. *Mais oui,* he says, my work *will* produce children! Children who will at least understand why they are afraid. How can a child be a child if she is afraid?

I cannot argue. Since the moment, as a small boy, Pierre heard of Tashi's dark tower and her terror of it, he has never put her suffering out of his mind. Everything he learns, no matter how trivial or in what context or with whom, he brings to bear on her dilemma. The conversations we have as adults predictably include some bit of information that he has stored away to become a part of Tashi's puzzle.

The only girl he ever loved, for instance. A Berkeley student with whom he often went horseback riding.

She rode bareback, always, he tells me, as we sit on a boulder in the park in the middle of an afternoon hike. She experienced orgasm while riding the horse.

Are you sure? I ask.

Yes, he says. She swooned. And when I asked her, she admitted it.

I am speechless at the thought that any woman's pleasure might be found so easily, I stammer; so, in a sense, *carelessly.*

The word you are looking for, says Pierre, is *wantonly. Loosely.* A woman who is sexually "unrestrained," according to the dictionary, is by definition "lascivious, wanton and loose." But why is that? A man who is sexually unrestrained is simply a man.

Well, I say, *was* she loose?

179

Pierre shifts his weight on the boulder and frowns up at the sky. Now, he says, in the scholarly tone that still strikes me as amusing in one so childlike in size, we can begin to understand something about the insistence, among people in mutilating cultures, that a woman's vagina be tight. By force if necessary. If you think of being wanton, being loose, as being able to achieve orgasm easily.

How did this happen? I ask. To your friend, I mean.

She'd been brought up by pagan parents, earth worshippers, on a little island somewhere in Hawaii. She could experience orgasm doing almost anything. She said that at home there were favorite trees she loved that she rubbed against. She could orgasm against warm, smooth boulders, like this one we're sitting on; she could come against the earth itself if it rose a bit to meet her. However, says Pierre, she'd never been with a man. Her parents had taught her early on that it wasn't absolutely necessary, unless she wanted to have children.

And with you? I ask.

I'm afraid my lovemaking had a dampening, no, a *drying* effect, he says. No matter how I tried, it was hard not to approach her from a stance of dominance. When making love with me, she became less and less wet. His face is sad for a moment, then he grins. She went off to India. I think she left me for an elephant she learned to ride, or perhaps for a slow, warm trickle of water from a waterfall, of which there were many amorous ones on her Hawaiian island.

I always thought perhaps it was to make sexual

love between women impossible that men destroyed their external sexual organs.

I still think that is partly true, says Pierre. But there is also my experience with Queen Anne.

Queen Anne? Your friend was named after Queen Anne Nzingha, the African warrior?

No, he says. After Queen Anne's lace, the wild-flower.

Later on in the hike, stopping at a pipe for water, Pierre still muses. Is it only woman who would make love to everything? he asks. Man too, after all, has external sexual organs. But does man seek oneness with the earth by having sex with it?

You mean Queen Anne wasn't simply masturbating?

No. She said she never masturbated, except with herself. And even then she was making love. Having sex. Her partner just happened to be something other than another human being.

Was it with Queen Anne that you discovered your duality? I ask.

Yes, he says. Until I met her I was never sexually attracted to women. I imagined all women mainly suffered from sex. Meeting her was a great relief. I realized that even bisexuality, of which I'd always felt myself capable but of which I'd had no real experience, was still, like homosexuality and hetero-sexuality, like lesbianism, only a very limited sexual-ity. I mean, here was someone who was *pan*sexual. Remember Pan? he asks, laughing. Well, Queen Anne was Pan's great-grandmother!

An image of Pan, the Greek god, merrily playing his flute in the forest rises up. His human head rests on a body composed of the parts of many different animals. Clearly his ancestors had related sexually, at least in imagination, to everything. And before him Queen Anne's ancestors had related sexually to the earth itself. I am really too old to use the expression "wow" gracefully. But "wow" is what I hear myself say. Which makes Pierre laugh again.

But in a moment he has returned to the thread of his thought. In pornography, he says ruefully, this ability of woman's to take pleasure in diverse ways is projected in a perverted way. I have seen films in which she is forced to copulate with donkeys and dogs and guns and other weapons. Oddly shaped vegetables and fruits. Broom handles and Coke bottles. But this is rape. Man is jealous of woman's pleasure, Pierre says after a while, because she does not require him to achieve it. When her outer sex is cut off, and she's left only the smallest, inelastic opening through which to receive pleasure, he can believe it is only his penis that can reach her inner parts and give her what she craves. But it is only his lust for her conquest that makes the effort worthwhile. And then it is literally a battle, with blood flowing on both sides.

Ah, I say, the original battle of the sexes!

Exactly, he replies.

Well, I say, some men turn to animals, and each other. Or they use the woman as if she were a boy.

If you are at all sensitive to another's pain, he says, grimacing, or even cognizant of your own, not to mention the humiliation of forcing yourself inside someone whose very flesh has been made into a barrier against you, what else can you do?

PART
THIRTEEN

Evelyn

For years I watched a television program called "Riverside." It was about a hospital for psychiatric disorders that reminded me of the Waverly. When Amy Maxwell was introduced to me by Raye, and closely resembled the woman who played the tough, compassionate matriarch and physician emeritus of the hospital, I felt immediately relaxed with her. She was elderly, bony and silver-haired, with a mouth full of straight white teeth which appeared to be wired into a permanent grin. She peered at me over silver half-glasses and stuck out her hand.

Raye sat as usual in her maroon wingback chair, a bemused look on her face. I could not fathom why Amy and I were being brought together. As a joke to myself I wondered: Could this woman be Mzee's belated bag of clay?

I learned something from Amy recently that I thought might interest you, said Raye, leaning forward.

There was a long silence, during which I was

185

highly conscious of the powdered pinkness of Amy's face and the mock-orange scent of her perfume. At last she began to speak. She spoke of her son, Josh—a word which in Olinka means turban—and of how he had been for many years a patient of Raye's. She spoke his name softly, tentatively, as if unsure she had a right to it. He had danced with a major ballet company throughout his twenties, after which he had had a hard time keeping up. Aging, out of work, depressed, he'd killed himself while still in his thirties.

Almost from birth he suffered from depression, said Amy. And almost from birth, she continued, with a self-deprecating look from Raye to me, I hauled him off to the shrink. Like the dutiful little soldier he was, he went unprotesting to have his head and heart examined by a succession of psychiatrists in an effort to adjust to my incessant cheerfulness: a sunniness so persistent it drove his father, a man of normal, up-and-down emotions, away. No matter what happened to me, I rose above it, said Amy, as my own mother had taught me to do, and as she herself had always done. She was a Southern belle in the Scarlett O'Hara mode. Poor for much of her life, but then fabulously wealthy finally because she married my father, who owned a lot of downtown New Orleans.

Here she paused and looked out the window. It was February; across the street the acacias were in bloom. The three of us were quiet, enjoying the look of the fine yellow fuzziness against the new and tender green. I was more puzzled than ever. I glanced sidelong at Raye, but she was sitting back in her

186

chair, her eyes warmly encouraging as she gazed at Amy's face. I realized this was not her first time hearing this.

Amy laced her thin fingers together and cleared her throat. How old was she? I wondered. Seventy-five? Eighty? Older? She seemed remarkably fit, whatever her age. It was only when he wound up here, with Raye, she said, that he began to suspect the depression he'd always carried was mine.

What do you mean? I said.

I mean, said Amy, sighing, that when I was a very little girl I used to touch myself . . . there. It was a habit that mortified my mother. When I was three years old she bound my hands each night before I was put to bed. At four she put hot pepper sauce on my fingers. At six years of age our family doctor was asked to excise my clitoris.

Is New Orleans America? I asked suspiciously. For this was all I could think to say.

Yes, said Amy, I assure you it is. And yes, I am telling you that even in America a rich white child could not touch herself sexually, if others could see her, and be safe. It is different today, of course. And even back then not every parent reacted as my mother did. But that I was not the only one this happened to I am sure.

I don't believe you, I said, rising to go. For I saw the healthy green leaves of my America falling seared to the ground. Her sparkling rivers muddy with blood.

Raye rose also and placed a hand on my arm. I was angry with her, and I knew the look in my eyes expressed it. How dare she subject me to such lies!

Wait, she said.

I sat.

Amy smiled, a small, modest smile, in spite of her tense mouth that was shaped into a wider grin. You think you are the only African woman to come to America, don't you? she asked.

Actually, I did think this. Black American women seemed to me so different from Olinka women, I rarely thought of their African great-great-grand-mothers.

Many African women have come here, said Amy. Enslaved women. Many of them sold into bondage because they refused to be circumcised, but many of them sold into bondage circumcised and infibulated. It was these sewed-up women who fascinated the American doctors who flocked to the slave auctions to examine them, as the women stood naked and defenseless on the block. They learned to do the "procedure" on other enslaved women; they did this in the name of Science. They found a use for it on white women . . . Amy laughed, suddenly. They wrote in their medical journals that they'd finally found a cure for the white woman's hysteria.

Well, somebody had to, said Raye, with a straight face. And the two of them actually sat there laughing.

I could not take it in. I stared at Amy.

It had been done to the grandmother of our cook, she said. Many operations, when she was a girl. She couldn't have children of her own; she'd adopted Gladys, my mother's childhood companion and maid, whose own clitoris had been excised; though she had not, like her mother, been infibulated. Gladys was docile in the extreme, not legally a slave, but superbly slavish in spirit. She just had no spunk. No self. This "gentleness of spirit," as my mother called it, was always held up as exemplary and the way my mother wanted me to be.

Raye and I watched as tears coursed down cheeks that even then held their grin shape. My first year in America, Adam and Olivia had taken me to the circus and there'd been a weeping clown with a wide white smile painted on his face. That was what Amy's face was like.

I was to be controlled all my life, she said, by my mother's invisible hand. And it *was* invisible, she cried, striking the arm of her chair with a clenched fist. Because I *forgot!*

You were a child, said Raye firmly. A child who was told your tonsils were being removed. A child who did not know such a thing as your mother did to you was possible. A child ignorant of what was so wrong about touching yourself. Too young to think something that felt so comforting could be wrong.

Amy wiped her eyes with a tissue. Sniffled. Her gray eyes were red, and appeared to perspire rather than tear.

I was sore for a long time, she said. My mother let me stay in bed and brought me lemonade to soothe my throat—for she convinced me it was my throat in which the work had been done and therefore where I felt the pain. And I could not touch my fingers to where the pain actually was, for fear of contradicting her. Or offending her. I never touched myself—in that way—again. And of course when I accidentally touched myself there I discovered there was nothing left to touch.

189

I became cheerful. I went in for sports because I enjoyed the high achieved by competitive exertion. My body was hard, lean, fit. Nothing missing. I had sex with practically anyone. Screwing madly, feeling nothing; in order not to feel my rage. I smiled even as, years later, I laid Mother in her grave. But I did not begin to remember until Josh died, when my own life was virtually over; because suddenly I had to start feeling my own feelings for myself. I had tried to live through Josh's body because it was whole. I'd pushed him to be a dancer; I can only imagine his sadness when he could no longer dance for me.

After this distressing conversation, from which I angrily extricated myself by slamming out of Raye's office, I ceased watching "Riverside." I now read everything I could find on Louisiana and New Orleans. I learned Louisiana had once belonged to France. Maybe, I thought, reliving the hostility anything French always provoked in me, Amy's mother had had trouble communicating with her doctor, who was perhaps like me a stranger from another tribe; perhaps her troubles stemmed from a complication encountered in the language. Perhaps Amy's mother had meant her daughter's tonsils after all.

PART
FOURTEEN

Evelyn-Tashi

Every day now, down below my window in the street, there are demonstrations. I can not see them, but the babble of voices rises up the wall of the prison and pours right through the iron bars.

What I am really hearing, says Olivia, is the cultural fundamentalists and Muslim fanatics attacking women who've traveled from all parts of the country to place offerings beneath the shrubbery that is just below and around the corner from my view. The women bring wildflowers, herbs, seeds, beads, ears of corn, anything they can claim as their own and that they can spare. They are mostly quiet. Sometimes they sing. It is when they sing that the men attack, even though the only song they all know and can sing together is the national anthem. They hit the women with their fists. They kick them. They swing at them with clubs, bruising the women's skins and breaking bones. The women do not fight back but scatter like hens; huddling in the doorways of shops up and down the street, until the shopkeepers sweep them back into the street with their brooms.

On the day I was sentenced to death the men did not bother the women, who, according to Olivia, simply sat, spent, hidden as much as they could be, at the base of the dusty shrubbery. They did not talk. They did not eat. They did not sing. I had not realized, before she told me of their dejection, how used I had become to their clamor. Even with my family beside me, cushioning the blow of the death sentence, without the noise of the battle from the street I felt alone.

But then, the next day, the singing began again, low and mournful, and the sound of sticks against flesh.

Benny

I can not believe my mother is going to die—and that dying means I will never see her again. When people die, where do they go? This is the question with which I pester Pierre. He says when people die they go back where they came from. Where is that? I ask him. Nothing, he says. They go back into Nothing. He wrote in huge letters in my notebook: NOTHING = NOT BEING = DEATH. But then he shrugged, that curious movement of his shoulders that caused my mother finally to like him, and wrote: BUT EVERYTHING THAT DIES COMES AROUND AGAIN.

I ask him if this means my mother will come back. He says, Yes, of course. Only not as your mother.

He said, Look at it this way. In the year nine hundred and twelve the people of Olinka had a stupid leader who put people to death by hanging. Now their stupid leader puts them to death by

shooting. Now he is driven everywhere in a Mer-
cedes. In nine hundred and twelve he was carried on
the shoulders of four strong slaves everywhere he
went. You see?

I did not.

Adam

When someone informs you your wife is to be assassinated publicly, it is a very bitter thing. I am always thinking of it, worrying it like a pip at the tip of my tongue. Olivia tells me not to read the papers, that they are filled with lies. I can not help it. I have become morbidly interested in this country's problems as they are revealed by inept and corrupt journalists. All the credible journalists have by now been beaten into silence, bought off, murdered, or chased into exile. The ones that are left have but one function: tell the people lies that flatter the president. In every edition of the two remaining papers there is a huge photograph of him: roundfaced, chuckleheaded, beaming like an evil moon. He is president for life, and that is that. The people are reminded over and over of his exploits as a youth against the white colonialists. They are told how, daily, he fights the neo-imperialists, who are still intent on stealing their country from them. They are told how frugally he husbands their dwindling resources and of how, during the latest interminable drought, he permits the lawn of his palace to be watered but once a week. Of course it is practically the only lawn in Olinka—lawns not being an African tradition—but no matter.

He has been rabid in his insistence on the death penalty for Tashi. It is said all of his wives, except for the one from Romania, were circumcised by M'Lissa. The few professional women who sought a meeting with him to beg for Tashi's life were turned away by his secretary and warned they would lose their jobs if they pressed their interest in the case further. There was a photograph of the women as they were dismissed. They looked ashamed, and their eyes did not meet the camera. One easily imagined their sliding feet.

At night I dream of Tashi as she was when she was a girl. In one of my dreams I recovered what was at one time a favorite expression of hers: But what *is* it? she would say, as my father or mother brought out some odd item they'd brought over or had sent to them from America. She'd never seen a kaleidoscope, for instance, and even while turning it round and round before her startled eye, and oohing and aahing at the fantastic colors and shapes it made, she would say, in a voice so filled with wonder it made us laugh: But what *is* it?

In my dream I see this child, scrawny, dusty, blood trailing her heels, approach the gallows. The noose dangles before her face, rapt and curious. It is placed round her neck by the president of the republic. Still she marvels, fingers it with reverence. But what *is* it? she cries, as the noose is tightened and she is dropped into oblivion.

Tashi-Evelyn

Now that justice is to be served and I am to be put to death, I am permitted visitors other than my family. One morning Olivia brings in the potters who are replicating the ancient fertility dolls.

But they are not fertility dolls, apparently. One of the women, as stout as I am now from my sedentary life and the starchy prison food, and as solid as a tree trunk, informs me that the word "doll" is derived from the word "idol." The figures that have come down to us as mere dolls were once revered as symbols of the Creator, Goddess, the Life Force Itself. She proffers a stack of photographs of paintings she has discovered among caves and rocks in the driest parts of the country. Where, when we were children, we were told witches and hobgoblins lived. The people who actually lived there, I discovered later on as an adult, were impoverished nomads who resisted being settled, and of whose filth and flies the government, which desperately imitated its British predecessors, was ashamed. In ancient times, says the potter, pursing her lips as if sucking on a seed, the people repainted the paintings year after year. She chuckled. They lived in a vast art gallery, one could say. Now—she grimaces—they are so faded as to be barely visible. Still, with effort, as I take one of the photographs from her hands, it is possible to recognize the little figure from M'Lissa's hut, smiling broadly, eyes closed, and touching her genitals. If the word "MINE" were engraved on her finger, her meaning could not be more clear. She is remarkably alive. Nor is she alone. Another photograph shows a figure with her hand around the penis of the figure next to her. She is also smiling. Another shows a figure with her finger in another woman's vagina. She too is smiling. So is the other woman. So, indeed, are they all. Other photographs show women figures dancing, interacting with animals, nestled cozily underneath sheltering trees, and giving birth.

We think children were given these "idols" to play with, as a teaching tool, says the other potter, in some age—she laughs—quite beyond the scope of the present imagination. And that when women were subjugated, these images were sent literally underground, painted on the walls of caves and sheltered enclosures of rock. Some of the stone and clay figures are of course in museums and private collections. The most famous one is of a man and a woman copulating, and his penis is huge; the woman appears to be impaled on it. This is an ancient image, and perhaps the reason all black penises were assumed by white people to be huge. She pauses. Many of the figures were destroyed. Especially those that show both a woman's vagina and her contented face. She shrugs. Now of course every little girl is given a doll to drag around. A little figure of a woman as toy, with the most vacuous face imaginable, and no vagina at all.

We are not supposed to have vaginas under this scheme, says Olivia, with a smartness of speech that sometimes characterizes her, because it is through that portal that man confronted the greatest undeserved mystery known to him. Himself reproduced.

The potters laugh.

I have a favorite, says the stout woman briskly, and takes from the bottom of the stack of photographs one in which three figures are joined, much like the three-monkey sculpture *See No Evil, Hear No Evil, Speak No Evil* that Adam's parents brought from America and kept on top of a cabinet in their kitchen. Except these figures—two women and a man—have their hands on their own sexual organs and on those of the others, their arms overlapping to form a kind of wedding band.

Thinking of it this way, as a marriage, and seeing the happy smiles on the fading visages of the fortunate three, I laugh. I can't help it. It is as if this sight strikes something awake that had been asleep, or dead, in my own body; though my body, alas, is now too damaged to respond to it in an uncorrupted way. I begin to sneeze.

But what *is* it? I hear myself finally, sneezing and laughing, say. And for me, the possibility of delight is once more dimly glimpsed in the world.

Olivia

Tashi says she wants to wear a red dress to face the firing squad. I remind her that her sentence is being appealed. There is also hope that the United States will honor her North American citizenship. I want to wear red anyway, she says, regardless of what happens. I am sick to death of black and white. Neither of those is first. Red, the color of woman's blood, comes before them both.

And so, we sew.

PART
FIFTEEN

Tashi-Evelyn

You do not know anything, said M'Lissa, as I brushed her hair. You keep asking, as only a fool does, about the people and events of your own time. I could tell you that red fingernail polish is all that remains of woman's recognition of her own blood power and you would not understand me. Or that red on a woman's mouth signals something other than a taste for meat. Here M'Lissa grunted suggestively.

In the old days before the people of Olinka were born as a people it is said that the blood of woman was sacred. And when women and men became priests blood was smeared on their faces until they looked as they had at birth. And that symbolized rebirth: the birth of the spirit. Myself, I was baptized by your husband's father, the missionary, and I bowed my head and held my tongue, for I knew their church's water was a substitute for woman's blood. And that they, who considered me ignorant, did not know this.

207

What, other than her lying life, did I want from M'Lissa? I worried this question incessantly, as only the insane can. Each night I fingered the razors I kept concealed in the stuffing of my pillow, fantasizing her bloody demise. I swore I would mutilate her wrinkled body so much her own God wouldn't recognize her. I smiled to think of her nose lying bloody on the bed. But each morning, like the storyteller Scheherazade, M'Lissa told me another version of reality of which I had not heard.

One day, as I was washing carefully between her clawlike toes, she informed me blandly that it was only the murder of the *tsunga,* the circumciser, by one of those whom she has circumcised that proves her (the circumciser's) value to her tribe. Her own death, she declared, had been ordained. It would elevate her to the position of saint.

This confession, or lie, stayed my hand for many a day.

M'Lissa

I know what young people can't even imagine or guess. That when one has seen too much of life, one understands it is a good thing to die.

The very first day she came I could see my death in Tashi's eyes, as clearly as if I were looking into a mirror. Those eyes that are the eyes of a madwoman. Can she really think I have not seen madness and murderers before?

In the village when I was a girl the mad were kept out in the bush. They lived alone in smelly, ramshackle huts, their filthy clothes in tatters. Their matted hair covering their backs like moss. I learned not to fear them, for I discovered, as all the villagers knew, that mad people, though murderous at heart, could, nonetheless, be easily distracted. If one lunged, you offered him or her—for there were always mad women and men; who never, incidentally, chose to live together—a yam. Or a song. Or a story that only a mad person could grasp the sense of. Stories we laughed at, nonsensical rhymes, made

them weep. Stories sorrowful to us, about our own
sufferings or those of the village, made them laugh
like the fiends they were. While they laughed or
cried, ate their yam or tried, usually without success,
to locate the stinkweed we'd stuck in their mossy
locks, off we ran.

To Tashi I have posed the following question, and
she has failed so far to properly answer it: Tashi, I
have said to her, it is clear you love your adopted
country *so* much; I want you to tell me, What does
an American look like?

Evelyn-Tashi

What does an American look like? the old witch has asked me. I started right in describing Raye. She is of a color not seen in Africa, I say. Except in certain seed pods or lightish brown kinds of wood. She has curly hair that is at the same time a bit nappy. Also never seen in Africa. And she has freckles. Also not seen in Africa. M'Lissa listens carefully and then questions shrewdly. Really? she asks. But is not America the land of the ghostly whites?

I hasten to describe Amy Maxwell. Her wired smile and powdery skin that is tinged with yellow and pink. Her bony shoulders and marble eyes. Her teased white hair. Her sorrow and hurt.

But M'Lissa is not satisfied.

I begin to describe people with yellow skin and slanted eyes. These, she scoffs, must be Eskimos, of

211

whom she has heard. Everyone knows they live far in the frozen north. Am I sure I can describe a real American?

I describe white men from television, with hearty voices and fake warmth in their eyes. I describe Indians from India and Native Americans from Minnesota. Red women with black hair. Yellow people with blue eyes. Brown people with black eyes who speak a language from another country.

M'Lissa waits.

It seems there is no answer to her question. Americans, after all, have come from so many places. This thought alone, I think, must boggle the mind of M'Lissa, who's never been anywhere.

If you say to someone in Africa: What does an Olinkan or a Maasai look like, there is an easy answer. They are brown or very brown. They are notably short (Olinkans) or tall (Maasai). But no, shortness or tallness, browness or redness, is not what makes an American.

Finally, outdone, but also sensing an ancient trick, I stopped this little game of hers, and brought us closer to the day of her death.

What does an American look like? she teased me complacently after several weeks had passed and I'd offered her hundreds of descriptions of Americans who rarely resembled each other physically and yet resembled each other deeply in their hidden histories of fled-from pain.

What does an American look like? I asked the question softly to myself, and looked M'Lissa in the eye. The answer surprised us both.

An American, I said, sighing, but understanding my love of my adopted country perhaps for the first time: an American looks like a wounded person whose wound is hidden from others, and sometimes from herself. An American looks like me.

PART
SIXTEEN

Tashi-Evelyn

The very first day after Mbati left, and I was required to wash M'Lissa, I saw why she was lame. Not only had her clitoris, outer and inner labia, and every other scrap of flesh been removed, but a deep gash traveled right through the tendon of her inner thigh. That was why, when walking, she had to drag her left leg. It was supported by the back tendon and the buttock muscles alone. Indeed, the left buttock was far more developed than the right, and even though she hadn't really walked with vigor in many years, there was a firm resilience in her flesh on that side.

Yes, touch it, my daughter, she exclaimed, as she felt my fingers exploring the keloidal tissue of the old wound, as hard as a leather shoe sole. It is the mark, on my body, of my own mother's disobedience.

Since this was the day on which I had earlier

217

resolved to kill M'Lissa, I was unsure whether
to appear interested in her life. That is, her life before she murdered Dura. But she was remembering,
and I had not completed her bath. Trapped, I
listened.

M'Lissa

Since the people of Olinka became a people there has always been a *tsunga*. It was hereditary, like the priests. Before the people became a tribe they lived too. But that was considered an evil time, because although everyone knew they had a mother, because she had given birth to them, a father was not to be had in the same way. You could not be sure. And so, your mother's brother was your father. The house always belonged, in those days, to the woman, and there were never children without parents or a home. But somehow this was seen as evil. Anyway, from the time of memory, always, in my family, the women were *tsungas*.

But why is that? I asked my mother.

Because it is such an honor, she replied. And also because it is the way we fill our bellies.

She was a sad woman, my mother. I never saw her smile.

She often prayed.

219

When I became old enough to be aware of her suffering, I began to notice that when she prayed, she faced a certain direction, and that she often went off, walking slowly, looking back over her shoulder as if she thought someone followed her, in the direction of her prayers.

Once, following her, I saw her enter a blighted forest where no one ever went, walk up to a hole in a rotting tree, and take something out of it. She unwrapped it, looked upon it, kissed it, and replaced it, all in a single motion. This forest was a kind of no-man's-land. Barren. Everything dry and dying. It was said this blight was caused long ago by a man and a woman fornicating there, when the area was planted in cereal grains. But this had happened so long ago no one remembered their fate, or even who they were.

After my mother had left, I crept up to the tree in which the small wrapped object lay, and took it carefully down into my lap, where I unwrapped it. It was a small smiling figure with one hand on her genitals, every part of which appeared intact. This was before I was circumcised, and so, with the ready curiosity of a child, I lay right down to compare my vulva to the little statuette's. Hidden behind a boulder, I very cautiously touched myself. The blissful, open look of the little figure had aroused me, and I felt an immediate response to my own touch. It was so sudden, so shocking and unexpected, it frightened me. I hastily rewrapped the little figure, placed it back in its niche, and ran.

I would often go back to the blighted place and

take the little figure down from the tree and play with it. But it seemed too powerful for me to ever again compare to myself. And so, I never again touched myself. If I had, then at least I would have known the experience that the work of the *tsunga* was trying to prevent.

Can you imagine the life of the *tsunga* who feels? I learned not to feel. You can learn not to. In this I was like my grandmother, who became so callous people called her "I Am a Belly." She would circumcise the children and demand food immediately after; even if the child still screamed. For my mother it was a torture.

Then, one day, my mother had to circumcise the girls in my age group.

Prior to that day, for weeks, she prayed to the little idol constantly. And when my turn came she tried to get away with cutting lightly. Of course she took the outer lips, because four strong eagle-eyed women held me down; and of course the inner lips too. But she tried to leave me a nub, down there where the charge I had felt with the little statuette had seemed to be heading. She barely nicked me there. But the other women saw.

What my mother started, the witchdoctor finished. He had learned all the healing and cures that he knew from women, which was why he was called a witchdoctor, and he wore the witch's grass skirt, but the witches who taught him had been put to death, because they refused circumcision and were too powerful among the women to be left free, uncircumcised. He showed no mercy. In fright and unbearable pain my body bucked under the razor-sharp stone he was cutting me with . . .

I could never again see myself, for the child that finally rose from the mat three months later, and dragged herself out of the initiation hut and finally home, was not the child who had been taken there. I was never to see that child again.

Tashi

And yet, I said, hardening myself against the sight of M'Lissa's heaving chest, expecting tears, you saw her over and over again, hundreds, thousands of times. It was she who screamed before *your* knife.

M'Lissa sniffled. I have never cried after that, she said. I knew in the moment when the pain was greatest, when it reached a crescendo, as when a loud metal drum is struck with a corresponding metal stick, that there is no God known to man who cares about children or about women. And that the God of woman is autonomy.

Cry, I said. Perhaps it will ease you.

But I could see that, even now, she could not feel her pain enough to cry. She was like someone beaten into insensibility. Bitter, but otherwise emotionally inert.

Why did they make us do it? she asked. I never really knew. And the women, even today, after giving birth, they come back to the *tsunga* to be resewn, tighter than before. Because if it is loose he won't receive enough pleasure.

But you taught them this, I said. It is what you told me. Remember? The uncircumcised woman is loose, you said, like a shoe that all, no matter what their size, might wear. This is unseemly, you said. Unclean. A proper woman must be cut and sewn to fit only her husband, whose pleasure depends on an opening it might take months, even years, to enlarge. Men love and enjoy the struggle, you said. For the woman . . . But you never said anything about the woman, did you, M'Lissa? About the pleasure she might have. Or the suffering.

I am weeping now, myself. For myself. For Adam. For our son. For the daughter I was forced to abort.

There *is* caesarean section, you know, the aborting doctor had said. But I knew I could not bear being held down and cut open. The thought of it had sent me reeling off into the shadows of my mind; where I'd hidden out for months. I watched from a lofty distance as Adam packed for his twice-yearly visits to Paris, to be with Lisette and his other son; I watched Benny struggle with all his might to be close to me, to melt into my body, to inhale my scent; and I was like a crow, flapping my wings unceasingly in my own head, cawing mutely across an empty sky. And I wore black, and black and black.

If I look at M'Lissa I know I will leap up and strangle her. Fortunately I am unable to move. I look down at my feet. Feet that hesitate before any nonflat surface: stairs, hills. Feet that do not automatically or nimbly leap over puddles or step gracefully onto curbs.

Perhaps an hour passes. I think M'Lissa has fallen asleep. I glance at the bed and am startled by how small she looks. She seems to have shrunk. I glance at her face. It is alert, watchful. But not because of me. She seems to have forgotten me.

I finally see her, she says, astonished. Self-absorbed.

Who? I ask. You finally see who?

She makes a slight dismissive motion with her hand, warning me not to interrupt.

The child who went into the initiation hut, she says. You know I left her there bleeding on the floor, and I came out. She was crying. She felt so betrayed. By everyone. They'd severely beaten her mother as well, and she blamed herself for this. M'Lissa sighed. I couldn't think about her anymore. I would have died. So I walked away, limped away, and just left her there. M'Lissa paused. Her voice when she continues is a whisper, amazed. She is still crying. She's been crying since I left. No wonder I haven't been able to. She has been crying all our tears.

M'Lissa

I have been strong. This is what I tell the tourists who come to see me, and the young mothers and the old mothers and everybody who comes. It is what they tell me back: the president and the politicians and the visitors from the churches and the schools. Strong and brave. Dragging my half-body wherever half a body was needed. In service to tradition, to what makes us a people. In service to the country and what makes us who we are. But who are we but torturers of children?

PART
SEVENTEEN

Tashi

Crowded into the small white chapel on the top floor of the prison are Adam, Olivia, Benny, Pierre, Raye and Mbati. Raye has flown in for the execution, though she denies it. It is not your death that is so fascinating, she says bluntly. It is still your life with which I am concerned. Besides, she says saucily, hands on her hips, You're not dead yet!

Indeed, I think, I am not. But neither would I say I am fully alive.

Considering the deterioration of the rest of the prison, says Mbati, it is odd that the chapel is still intact.

That's because no one uses it, says Adam, fingering the dusty unopened Bible, whose gilt-edged pages have been gnawed by moths.

It is even cool here, in the evenings; the windows are large and nothing, not even shutters, blocks the breeze. There are no bars, presumably because it is too high to jump.

229

Since the trial, Olivia has volunteered to work mornings downstairs on the AIDS floor. Adam, Benny and Pierre have rented a jeep and explored the countryside. We've filmed everything, says Benny, and now we want you to see it.

Adam starts the projector; at first there are slides. Pictures of the northern territory and its petroglyphs and faded paintings of celebrations and hunts. But then there is a film. I know they are trying to prepare me for it because Olivia is suddenly handing me a glass of water and Adam is holding my hand.

Pierre, who has said he wants to be the first anthropologist to empower and not further endanger his subjects, now stands quietly beside the machine.

At first I think they are showing me a human settlement, a village. The shapes are the same. Huts with umbrella-shaped tops. Huts like mushrooms. But then there is a close-up of the "huts" and a man's feet and legs rising above them. I recognize Adam's hiking boots. Then, when the picture is opened up, I see that the settlement is vast, but the "huts" are tiny, only three to six inches high.

Hah, says Adam, squeezing my hand. Fooled you!

I thought it was a village, I say, turning to Olivia and Mbati. Didn't you?

Mbati smiles. Olivia says, Yes, I did. Though I did wonder about that short lumpy hut that leaned so drastically to the left.

But what is . . . , I start to say, but am choked by the desperate surge of my heart as it makes a sudden attempt to leave my chest.

It's ok, says Adam. You are not alone. We are all here with you.

You're not alone. You're not, you're not, I hear from Raye. Her perky voice seems to come to me from another age. Women who are not gelded have a different sound, I think. They can sound perky. A gelded woman can not.

I think this in a flash. My mind is despairing flight from the sight of a tall, rough, earthcolored column on the screen before me, Benny, dwarfed beside it, smiling uncertainly into the camera. My bag of clay! I think.

Pierre clears his throat. It is my belief, he says, after stopping the projector on the image before us, that human beings in Africa (the first ones on the planet, it is assumed), because of the heat and humidity, imitated the termite when they looked about for housing that would be comfortable, long-lasting and easily built. That is why many traditional African houses, even today, and all adobe houses anywhere, resemble those of termites. It was termites who taught early humans about natural air-conditioning, with their long vaulted passageways and great domed storage rooms. Termite houses, like mosques, are always cool, no matter what the out-side temperature. Termite houses are made from the earth itself, from clay, the cheapest and most plentiful substance around.

What surprises me is that I can hear Pierre, and even understand what he is saying. It is true my heart leapt painfully once, but now it is beating normally. I glance around the room at the faces gathered about me. They are each as intent as my own.

I look at Pierre and think: Yes, it is a good thing that we train our children to help us. We who need so much help. I send a flash of gratitude to those schools I've never set foot in, Berkeley and Harvard. If I should live, I think, I would visit them as shrines.

I believe, he continues, that over time there was a strong identification with the termite, which Africans call "white ant" even though it bears little resemblance to an ant. Unlike the ant, and most other insects, the termite has kept a place for males in its society. There is a queen, but also a king. Perhaps this is why, also, the people felt an affinity for it. White ants, as you know, are eaten by the people in the country, who prefer them fried.

And in the city too, if they could get them, says Olivia. She glances sharply at Mbati. It is disgusting to see how the youth are gorging on potato chips!

Adam laughs. Mbati pushes her bag of Fry-O potato chips deep in her string bag.

Their religious symbology became completely reflective of termite behavior, continues Pierre. Their gratitude, for having been taught so much by the termite, was great.

And of course the termite was so *delicious,* says Raye.

The termites, continues Pierre, would have taught them to make pots, which would have led inevitably to the notion that the first human beings were themselves fashioned out of clay. And that something or someone so fashioned them.

But, says Pierre, running slender brown fingers through his sunbleached dark curls, not to run on and on about this . . . This, Madame Johnson, is your dark tower. You are the queen who loses her wings. It is you lying in the dark with millions of worker termites—who are busy, by the way, maintaining mushroom farms from which they feed you —buzzing about. You being stuffed with food at one end—a boring diet of mushrooms—and having your eggs, millions of them, constantly removed at the other. You who are fat, greasy, the color as you have said of tobacco spit, inert; only a tube through which generations of visionless offspring pass, their blindness perhaps made up for by their incessant if mindless activity, which never stops, day or night. You who endure all this, only at the end to die, and be devoured by those to whom you've given birth.

Ah, says Olivia. The termite as Christ!

But how did I know this? I ask my little band of intent faces. No one told me.

We think it was told you in code somehow, says Raye. Not told you directly that you, as a woman, were expected to reproduce as helplessly and inertly as a white ant; but in a culture in which it is mandatory that every single female be systematically desexed, there would have to be some coded, mythological reason given for it, used secretly among the village elders. Otherwise they'd soon not know what they were talking about. Even today there are villages where an uncircumcised woman is not permitted to live. The chiefs enforce this. On the other hand, circumcision is a taboo that is never discussed. How then do the chiefs know to keep it going? How is it talked about?

My mind is blank. Surely no one ever told me anything except that . . . this thing M'Lissa did to me expressed my pride in my people; and that without it no man would marry me.

Perhaps, says Raye, you had a nursery rhyme when you were small, as innocuous as "Peter, Peter, pumpkin eater / Had a wife and couldn't keep her / Put her in a pumpkin shell / And there he kept her very well."

What? asks Benny. Puzzled.

It is about keeping a woman pregnant, says Pierre, stretching out his arms and curving them into a pumpkin shape. Enslaved by her own body.

Oh, says Benny. Appalled.

We know, from Griaule's work, that among the Dogon it was precisely the elders who were the guardians of the knowledge of the beginning of man. The Creation itself began with mutilation and rape . . . I wonder if you remember our little lesson, from Griaule's book, Madame Johnson, Pierre says, looking at me.

Much to my surprise, I do remember it. God wanted to have intercourse with the woman, I say. And the woman fought him. Her clitoris was a termite hill, rising up and barring his way.

Good, says Pierre.

Oh my God, says Raye. I know this sounds ridiculous, but the erect clitoris sort of resembles a little termite hill, or house.

Well, says Pierre, pointing to the giant one on the screen beside which Benny is standing, one like that clearly resembles a phallus.

When the clitoris rose, I continue, God thought it looked masculine. Since it was "masculine" for a clitoris to rise, God could be excused for cutting it down. Which he did. Then, I said, God fucked the hole that was left. Of course I remember, I say to Pierre, that Griaule said God had intercourse. It is I who say God fucked.

And this is how people who mutilate little girls see the beginning of life, groans Olivia, dropping her head into her hands.

Religion is an elaborate excuse for what man has done to women and to the earth, says Raye, bitterly.

But there were other religions, I say, thinking of the little figure blissfully loving herself.

Pierre shrugs. They were destroyed. Your little smiling goddess was destroyed.

I turn to Mbati. Her lovely face is filled with horror. Nobody knows this story, she says. I am convinced. Which means, she says, visibly angry, nobody even knows why they do this thing. I certainly never had any idea why it was done to me. If my sex organs were unclean, why was I born with them? I asked my mother this once, before I was circumcised. She just said everyone knew a woman's vulva to be dirty. And to need to be removed. That was all there was to it. No termites, no "white ants," no structural similarities between genitals and insect dwellings were discussed. And who would not laugh at the notion that a clitoris, like a penis, can rise?

Olivia asks if I am hungry or would like more water to drink. I am not sure. The sight of Mbati's anger has split me in two. Only a part of me is sitting in the midst of my family and friends. Another part is watching myself as a small child bring a tray of food and water to the elders of the village. They sit beside a baobab tree and gaze wisely out over the plain. The heat is intense but does not bother me. The earth is red. There are flies. Because I am small, they do not completely stop their talk.

Number one: What is a man?

All: Huh!

Number two: A man is blind.

All: Huh!

Number three: He has an eye.

All: Huh!

Number four: But it can not see.

Number one: Man is God's cock.

Number two: It scratches the furrow.

Number three: It drops the seed.

Number four: But its offspring . . .

All: The crop!

Number one: Excrement!

Number two: It cannot identify.

Number three: God's blind cock produces God's blind eggs.

Number four: Is an egg not blind?

Number one: It is so.

Number two: The *tsunga*'s stitch helps the cock to know his crop . . .

All: Which after all belongs to God.

Number three: That is why it is said . . .

Number four: . . . the *tsunga* though herself a woman . . .

Number one: . . . helps God.

All: Is it not so?

All: It is so.

All: Woman is Queen.

Number one: She is Queen.

Number two: God has given her to us.

Number three: We are thankful to God for all His gifts.

(They do not, however, thank the child for bringing the food or send thanks to her mother for preparing it.)

Number four: Since God has given her to us, we must treat her well.

Number one: We must feed her so that she will stay plump.

Number two: Even her excrement will be plump. (They laugh.)

Number three: If left to herself the Queen would fly.

Number two: True.

Number three: And then where would we be?

Number four: But God is merciful.

Number one: He clips her wings.

Number two: She is inert.

Number three: And even her excrement is sweet. (Laughter)

Number four: Because she is Queen!

Number one: And we are only workers!

Number two: Blind, it is true, but that is God's will.

Number three: Did He not make us so?

Number four: True.

Number one: And did He not put the Queen's body there to make our offspring?

Number two: And to be our food?

Number three: It can not be denied.

Number four: And when she rose up . . .

All: Hah!

Number three: Rose up indeed.

237

Number four: As a man would!

Number one: She did not see God's axe.

Number two: No, she was blind like us then. She did not see it.

Number three: God struck the blow that made her Queen!

Number four: Beautiful enough for him to fuck.

Number one: God liked it fighting!

(Laughter)

Number two: God liked it tight!

Number three: God liked to remember what He had done, and how it felt before it got loose.

Number four: God is wise. That is why He created the *tsunga.*

All: With her sharpened stone and bag of thorns!

Number one: With her needle and thread.

Number two: Because He liked it tight!

Number three: God likes to feel big.

Number four: What man does not?

(Laughter)

Number one: Let us eat this food, and drink to the Queen who is beautiful, and whose body has been given us to be our sustenance forever.

(Laughter, and the noisy eating of food)

The small child that I was is not noticed at all. She could have been a fly, or an ant. I do not particularly notice them, either. They've always been there underneath the baobab tree, graybearded, old. Dressed in thick dark robes against the sun. Their wise old heads wrapped and their eyes mirroring the timeless vacancy of the landscape around them.

Gazing at them now from the safety of the prison chapel, from the safety of my impending death, I can see they are shells, empty of life. It is they who are being stuffed with food, while nothing but oppressive verbal diarrhea comes out. The child, taught to respect these elders above all others, could not have recognized this. The old men discussing her and all the females of the village did not care that she heard them. They knew she would not be able to figure out what they were talking about. They were discussing her, determining her life, and at the time she did not, could not, know. And yet, there in her unconscious had remained the termite hill, and herself trapped deep inside it, heavy, wingless and inert, the Queen of the dark tower. From my seat in the chapel, Adam's hand still in mine, I glance down at the feet of the child as she leaves the old men, belching in contentment, sitting in the dust. Idly, she kicks a stone. There is grace in her aim and no hesitation in her thrust.

PART
EIGHTEEN

Evelyn-Tashi

But what did you think, I ask M'Lissa. When I came into the Mbele camp asking to be "bathed."

I thought you were a fool, she says without hesitation. The very biggest.

But why? I ask.

Because, first of all, there were no other women in the camp. Didn't you have eyes in your head? Didn't anyone ever teach you that the absence of women means something? Or were you so wrapped up in yourself you didn't notice?

You were there, I say. And you told me the other women were all out on raids of liberation.

Huh! she scoffs. I lied. It was the camp itself that needed liberation. When the women came they were expected to cook and clean—and be screwed—exactly as they had been at home. When they saw how things were, they left. Even I would have left, M'Lissa says, glancing down at her lame leg.

Suddenly she laughs.

They sent for me, you know, just as they sent for

243

you. I was also sent a donkey to ride. They were constructing a traditional Olinkan village from which to fight, and therefore needed a *tsunga.*

They sent for me?

To give the *tsunga* something to do. To give the new community a symbol of its purpose.

Which I became, I say, dumbstruck.

Which you became, M'Lissa hisses. Lying on your mat of straw, making other little mats of straw. The same work your great-great-grandmother would have done!

But you encouraged it, I say, puzzled and hurt.

Do fools need encouragement? she asks the ceiling. They encourage themselves.

But Our Leader informed us . . . I think rapid thoughts with which to defend myself. But M'Lissa is quicker.

Did Our Leader not keep his penis? Is there evidence that even one testicle was removed? The man had eleven children by three different wives. I think this means the fellow's private parts were intact.

I am horrified to hear such a disrespectful view of Our Leader. M'Lissa, I say, behind that face you show to those who come asking about tradition, you are bitter.

Even the sweetest mango in my mouth is bitter to me, she says. But *women,* she sneers, women are too cowardly to look behind a smiling face. A man smiles and tells them they will look beautiful weeping, and they send for the knife.

They have reason to be afraid, I say. You, especially, cannot deny this.

Their biggest fear is that they will have to kill their sons, she says angrily. Even if they themselves almost died the first time a man broke into their bodies, they want to be told it was a minor hurt, the same that all women feel, that their daughters will barely notice, and cease, over time, to remember. If I tell them that, it makes it almost possible for them not to completely despise their sons.

For the pain they inflict.

Yes. Breaking into someone else's daughter. Just as another woman's son breaks into theirs.

But the sons know nothing of what is done to women. They only know they're supposed to be men enough to break into the woman's body. They often hurt themselves trying. I learned this from Adam, I say, whose father used to treat them for bruises and lacerations.

M'Lissa looks at me coolly.

I squirm under her gaze.

It was also very hard for Adam and me, I say. You'd sewed me so tight, an ant would have had difficulty crawling in.

Oh, M'Lissa says, You were not so tight as that! There are women walking around today who've paid the *tsunga*s to make them tighter than that! After each birth of a child they do it. More than once, more than twice, more than three times, they've had it done. Each time tighter than before.

But it hurts so much, I say.

The bitches are used to it, she says. And it is true, you know, the men like it tight. Fighting. Don't think the women never receive pleasure, either, says M'Lissa.

I never have, I say.

That is your own fault, she says. The pleasure a woman receives comes from her own brain. The brain sends it to any spot a lover can touch.

Then why is it that it is a woman's vulva that is destroyed? I ask. "Bathed," as they say, "cleaned off," I ask. And not her shoulders or her neck? Not her breasts?

While M'Lissa is pondering this, I recall the feeling of a banished sensation.

I did have pleasure, once or twice, after my "bath," I say.

Yes? she says.

But my pleasure shamed me.

Ah, says M'Lissa, your man gave it to you from behind. What is shameful about that? That is how boys do it to each other while waiting for the girl's dowry to be raised. Dowry raising takes such a long time, what can you expect them to do?

My pleasure angered me, I say. It made me hate my husband.

It was pleasure, wasn't it?

I felt I had been made into something other than myself.

You had been made into a woman! says M'Lissa. It is only because a woman is made into a woman that a man becomes a man. Surely you know that!

My husband was a man already.

True, says M'Lissa, but perhaps he did not know it.

PART
NINETEEN

Olivia

In the prison, now that the date of execution is set—the appeal failed; no word from America—Tashi is treated less like a condemned murderer and more like an honored guest. Within the prison she is permitted freedom. Her days are busy. There are visits from women's groups and the foreign press. Photographers from every part of the world come to snap her picture.

Through it all, she flourishes, her alert face kind and reflective, angry and disgusted by turns. Each morning she works with me on the AIDS floor, feeding, bathing or simply touching the patients. It is so crowded there's barely room to squat between mats. Adam and the boys have taken responsibility for feeding the children; bringing in hot meals from the kitchen of our rented house. This is a relief to their parents and older siblings, those that are left, and they thank us gravely with their eyes.

No one has any idea why he or she is sick. That's the most difficult thing. Witnessing their incomprehension. Their dumb patience, as they wait for death. It is their animal-like ignorance and acceptance that most angers Tashi, perhaps because she is reminded of herself. She calls it, scornfully, the assigned role of the African: to suffer, to die, and not know why.

Why, she wants to know, do mainly homosexual men and intravenous drug users get the disease in America, while here there are as many women dying as men? Who infects the children? Why are there more little girls dying than boys?

Among the wealthy Olinkans there is widespread denial that anything is wrong. They keep their dying relatives at home. It is mainly the poor we see. A gaunt mother staggers in, her emaciated, fifty-pound husband on her back, her children trailing behind. If there is room on the floor—if someone has died during the night—she and her family receive that space. If no one has died, she must make a space somehow in the hallway or on the landing of the stairs. People die quickly, once they get here, having waited so long before seeking help. That becomes a blessing for those faced with destitute victims who've traveled great distances in search of medicine and cure.

By now they know there is no cure. And no medicine, either, other than food, which is in short supply. Watery porridge twice a day.

Among the students who've been stricken there is a belief in all kinds of plots against them, hatched by foreigners. Or by their own government. It is bitter to watch them die: their country's future doctors, dentists, carpenters and engineers. Their country's fathers and mothers. Teachers. Dancers, singers, rebels, hellraisers, poets.

Adam spends most of his time talking with the students, the intellectuals. He tells them he has heard that people in a neighboring country were first infected by scientists who injected them with a contaminated vaccine against polio. The vaccine had been made from cultures taken from the kidneys of the green monkey. The vaccine, though presumably a prophylactic against polio, had not been purified, and carried with it the immune deficiency virus that causes AIDS.

One dying student disagrees with this. That's not the story I heard, he says. I heard Africans caught AIDS not from the green monkey's kidney but from his teeth! There are helpless derisive snorts at this modern version of the dog-bites-man story. The intellectuals conclude it must have been an experiment, like the one conducted on black men in Alabama, who were injected with the virus that causes syphilis, then studied as they sickened and died. The kind of experiment that would not have been hazarded on European or white American subjects. That they die holding this belief, that an African life is made for experiments, and is expendable, is almost more than I can bear.

Tashi is convinced that the little girls who are dying, and the women too, are infected by the unwashed, unsterilized sharp stones, tin tops, bits of glass, rusty razors and grungy knives used by the *tsunga*. Who might mutilate twenty children without cleaning her instrument. There is also the fact that almost every act of intercourse involves tearing and bleeding, especially in a woman's early years. The opening that is made will never enlarge on its own, but must always be forced. Because of this, infections and open sores are commonplace.

The anal intercourse kills women too, Adam says sadly one day, after a sweet-faced, woeful-eyed young woman has died. Her husband, distraught, and also stricken with the disease, explained to Adam that although they had been married three years they had no children because he had been unable to sleep with her as a man does normally with his wife. She had cried so, and bled. He had loved her, he said, but not like a man. His fear of causing her pain, he said, had cost them children. He had no understanding that the way in which he had made love to her had cost her, and him, her life. Though she was but one wife, of four, the number sanctioned by Islam and the Prophet, still it had been as though she were the only wife he had, he said, weeping. Because she alone had been capable of making him laugh. Even her name, Hapi, had sounded, he thought, something like the American word for fun.

Olivia

But why did you confess? I ask Tashi. I know you didn't do it. You couldn't have.

Olivia, she says, laughing with all her teeth, it would kill me to get any older. There is nothing more of this life I need to see. What I have already experienced is more than enough. Besides, she says soberly, maybe death is easier than life, as pregnancy is easier than birth.

Tashi

But Tashi, Olivia says, clinging to my neck. Don't do this to yourself. Don't do it to your son. Don't do it to Adam. Don't do it to me.

Olivia, I say, listen to yourself. Surely you remember having said those words to me before.

She looks blank.

When I was on the donkey, half-naked, I remind her. On my way to the Mbele camp.

Yes, she fairly shouts. And look what *happened.* You've paid for not listening to me all your life.

And I intend to keep on paying, I say.

But why? she asks. Forgive me for saying so, please. But it seems so stupid.

Because when I disobey you, the outsider, even if it is wrong, I am being what is left of myself. And that silver of myself is all I now have left.

They'll kill you, she says. And you are innocent!

Well, I say. Yes and no.

I am puzzled, she says, frowning.

You are right, Olivia, that I did not kill M'Lissa. I

254

am grateful, I say, for your confidence in me. M'Lissa did die under her own power, which, even at the end, was considerable; she seemed to get stronger, rather than weaker, with age. Hers was an evil power, barely acquainted, any longer, with good. It is for not killing her—in the name of the suffering she caused—that I am guilty. I do not, by the way, want this known.

What? That you didn't kill her? But why?

Because women are cowards, and do not need to be reminded that we are.

M'Lissa

The death of your sister—what was her name?—was your stupid mother Nafa's fault. It was not absolutely sure the chief would make us return to circumcision. After all, he was always grinning into the faces of the white missionaries and telling them he was a modern man. Not a barbarian, which he could have been, for they called the "bath" barbaric. He was chief, they said, he could stop it. Or was he chief? So of course he stopped it, to prove to them he was chief. His decision had nothing to do with us. One heard his own wives screaming when their time came. Did he care? No. Every man's wife screamed at the appropriate time.

Her name, I say, was Dura. She was small, thin; there was a crescent-shaped scar just above her lip; when she smiled it seemed to slide into her cheek.

I could lie, says M'Lissa, and tell you I remember her. After all the years I did this work, faces are the

256

last thing I remember. If she'd been hermaphroditic, then perhaps.

No, I say. I believe she was normal.

It is all normal, as far as that goes, says M'Lissa. *You* didn't make it, so who are you to judge?

I am nobody, I say. You made sure of that.

Stop feeling sorry for yourself! she says. You are like your mother. If Dura is not bathed, she said, no one will marry her. She never seemed to notice no one had ever married me, and that I lived anyway. This was even before the white missionaries left. Being bathed did not kill me, she said. And my husband has always been patient with me. Well, M'Lissa snorts, your father spread himself among six wives; he could afford patience.

As soon as she heard the new missionaries were black, she felt certain the village would be returned to all its former ways and that uncircumcised girls would be punished. She could not imagine a black person that was not Olinkan, and she thought all Olinkans demanded their daughters be bathed. I told her to wait. But no. She was the kind of woman who jumps even before the man says boo. Your mother helped me hold your sister down.

Stop, I say. Even if she were lying, as I now knew she often did, I could not bear to hear it.

But she says, No, I will not stop. You are mad, but you are not mad enough. Don't you think your mother might have told you how Dura died? She didn't, did she? That she was that one in a hundred girls so constructed that the slightest scratch made her bleed like a stuck cow. She had noticed this herself, from trying to stop the bleeding of the

257

scratches your sister got while playing. When I bathed you, this was something of which I thought.

And yet you said nothing, I say, though you might have killed me just as you killed Dura.

You'd come so far, and were so foolish, says M'Lissa. Besides, by then I did not care.

PART
TWENTY

Adam

Father, hear my confession.

It is in vain that I tell the young man I am not a priest. He has been waiting among the rest to die, since we first visited Tashi in the prison. His face is covered with purple lesions, his head is bald, his slight frame little more than bones. What distinguished him from the beginning, when I hunkered down to speak to him, was his insistence that he was a medical student: "With many years in university," he'd said, with a weak, superior flutter of his hand. This, and the fact that as he grew even weaker, his large brown eyes bruised with fear, he took to drawing himself up on his haunches and crossing his elbows on top of his head. He would remain in this odd position, whimpering, for hours; until he fell over in weariness or was pushed over by someone moving past.

I had always resisted intimacy with the victims. It was as if my heart, under the burden of my own

261

suffering, and having already witnessed so much human devastation, had gone numb.

However: My name is Hartford, he said, with a grimness to match my own. And yet, because of the unexpected associations evoked by his name (an elk, an American city in Connecticut and an insurance company), I smiled. He seemed charmed, as a child might be, by this response, and appeared to savor it, as a little child might a sweet. Wonderingly he withdrew the clawlike hand that had snagged my sleeve, and placed it against his own cracked, unsmiling lips.

Everything he said and did was in slow motion; it was several minutes before he spoke again.

In the old days, he said, whispering, there was more harmony in the world between man and creature. I have heard this said: in truth, how can I know? In the not so old days we people were hunted down and killed or stolen from our land and families to work for other people far across the sea. Hunted we were, like we hunt the monkey and the chimpanzee.

Here Hartford groaned and closed his eyes. Bubbles of perspiration burst on his skin. It was as if, suddenly, his body became a fountain. I mopped his skin with the tattered towel I carried with me, and when the sweating stopped, placed my hand on his swollen knee, which, protruding beneath the skin of his leg, was like a black coconut.

Father, he said, I am not a medical student. That is a lie I have told to salvage my self-respect.

I patted his knee, somehow startled at the intensity of his remorse; how difficult it was for him to disgorge these few words of shame. Besides, I honestly did not care.

Being a medical student, becoming a doctor, was only a dream I had, he sighed. When the pharmaceutical company offered us local boys "positions" in their factory, I thought my dream was on the way to becoming reality.

We did not know anything about these men. They were strange. They always wore white, so that they looked like the doctors we saw in films and on TV. They did not see you when they looked, that we knew. We felt we did not exist to them any more than they did to us. We could feel how strange we were to them, as well. We had always hunted monkeys and chimpanzees, they reminded us. What they were asking was nothing new. Only now there would be money, and, of course, often there would be meat. Both to eat and to sell.

So it began.

At first I was in the rainforest, hunting with the other boys. We loved our guns. We trapped and dragged back to the factory more monkeys and chimps than I'd even thought there were. I grew to identify, and sometimes mimic, chimp and monkey behavior. Monkey gestures. The mother always placed the baby behind her body, the little one's arm reaching around to her breast; the father always fought, then screeched a warning to others as he ran away. If we captured his mate and child, he would often follow so closely and with such disregard for his own safety it was easy to shoot him. This we often did, laughing.

He was not needed anyway. We were told this by

the pharmaceutical company, but we soon saw it for ourselves. Only the females and the babies were wanted. Very soon, no new monkeys or chimps were needed because the factory was at last complete. The local boys and I had filled it. With the help of only a few males, the females were forced to breed. This they did in cages hardly large enough for the act of mating.

Hartford swallowed. I held a glass of sweetened water to his lips. Suddenly his eyes rolled back in his head and his head dropped to one side. His pulse, when I took his arm, was faint as the heartbeat of an embryo.

At last he opened his eyes.

They were being raised for their kidneys, he said slowly, in a flat tone. Now that there was no longer a need to hunt them, I was assigned the job of decapitating them.

He paused, his eyes stormy, strong, and large enough to swallow me.

The screaming of monkeys, he said, musingly, studying my face as if he'd read a subtle change in me, is really unlike the scream of the peacock, which, as you know, is very human. But somehow, because of the chimps' and monkeys' faces, their screaming is even more human. Everything they think, everything they fear, everything they feel, is as clear as if you'd known them all your life. As if they'd slept in the same bed as you!

Do not disturb yourself, I said, gently, and still with a certain detachment. Even this horror could not penetrate to the level of numbness at which I dwelled. After all, I thought, how could he have

POSSESSING THE SECRET OF JOY

anticipated the evil of civilization, having been indoctrinated from birth to believe it the only future.

The factory was vast, he said. Vast. For they were manufacturing vaccine to sell to the whole world. I discovered this when I read some of the literature they received written in English. Most of it was written in some other language. Perhaps German or Dutch. On the other hand, there were often Americans about. Australians and New Zealanders. Hearty fellows, always enthusiastic; as if they were on the track of a cure for all mankind.

A fit of coughing now shook Hartford's emaciated frame. A spray of blood and mucus covered the rag I held to his mouth.

I had smiled jauntily, myself, the first year I worked for them, he said, as he lay back, resting, after the coughing fit. We were paid good money, and of course we ate or sold those animals who became —usually out of concern for their stolen families— meat. But soon I could not smile. I stood kneedeep in monkey heads, chimpanzee torsos . . .

Small boys with small knives were trained to make the slit . . . and haul the kidneys out. It was on these kidneys the men in white coats grew their precious "cultures."

The vaccine left the factory at the other end from where the monkeys and chimps were raised and slaughtered. It left in small clear bottles with blinding white labels and shiny metal caps.

As Hartford's voice became barely audible, a whispery rasp, an unbidden glimpse of what he was describing invaded my mind. I closed my eyes tightly to banish the sight. It was too late. I felt as if a whole

265

other world of grief and disaster had just been dropped on my soul. I groaned in agony, almost exactly as he had done. The sound of my own sorrow was shocking to me. But, surprisingly, my sorrow made Hartford look, finally, *released.*

Father, thank you for hearing my confession, he said, savoring my pained expression with the same wonder with which he'd enjoyed my smile. As if he'd waited until certain he had transmitted the full horror of his existence to someone who could still feel, Hartford began to breathe the shallow, rustling wheeze everyone on the AIDS floor knew so well.

There were things to do. In the morning I would lose my wife and friend forever. Where were my sons? I wondered. Or my sister, Olivia, for that matter; whom, I suddenly realized, I had always depended on to be the feeling side of me; it was she who had first noticed the weeping that would stain my wife's life. Perhaps they were with Tashi. I could not move to look for them. I sat where I was until, an hour after the death rattle began, Hartford—whose African name was perhaps lost forever—medical student and killer of monkeys and chimps, was dead.

Though not a priest, I am a man of God, even now. I could not bear a life lived without belief. But this I know: There is for human beings no greater hell to fear than the one on earth.

Tashi-Evelyn-
Mrs. Johnson

I confessed because I grew weary of the trial. Sick of sitting next to my attorney. He was always so dapper; so impeccably dressed. Smelling of Aramis. Loving the sound of his own mouth. The opposing attorney annoyed me as well.

I am old enough to be your grandmother, I thought, watching him prance and preen; and you stand there arguing for my death. In truth, it made me pity him, and see him as a fool.

I said to my attorney, in a moment when he was not twirling with a beringed finger one of his greasy curls, Let me take the stand. Though he was against my doing so, I took it anyway. As soon as I was seated, even before the Bible was brought, I said loud and clear so there could be no mistake: I did it.

How did you do it, Mrs. Johnson? asked the judge nearest me.

That, I said, is none of your damn business.

But do you think my confession stopped the trial? No, it did not. For days afterward they were still talking about finding my razors in the ashes of M'Lissa's house, and speculating on the gory ways I chose to mutilate and dispose of her. Their imaginations, I found, were even sicker than my own.

PART
TWENTY-ONE

Tashi-Evelyn

It is from Mbati that I learn the African does not call his or her house a "hut."

"Hut," she says, is Dutch for "cottage," and Africans are not Dutch.

I am this child's mother. Otherwise she would not have appeared so vividly, a radiant flower of infinite freshness, in my life.

In the evenings she reads aloud passages from books for us to puzzle over or enjoy. Tonight she reads from the book of a white colonialist author who has lived all her life among Africans and failed to see them as human beings who can be destroyed by suffering. "Black people are natural," she writes, "they possess the secret of joy, which is why they can survive the suffering and humiliation inflicted upon them."

Mbati stares at me blankly. I return her look.

But what *is* it? I ask. This secret of joy of which she writes. You are Black, so am I. It is of us then that she speaks. But we do not know. Or, I say, admiring her beauty, perhaps you do know.

Mbati laughs. Well, she says, we are *women*. We must find out! Especially since she also claims to understand the code of "birth, copulation and death" by which we live!

Oh, I say. These settler cannibals. Why don't they just steal our land, mine our gold, chop down our forests, pollute our rivers, enslave us to work on their farms, fuck us, devour our flesh and leave us alone? Why must they also write about how much joy we possess?

Mbati has never asked whether I murdered M'Lissa. She doesn't seem to care.

I am miserably flawed, I say to her as she is leaving, after she has promised not to let me die before she has discovered and presented to my eyes the *definitive* secret of joy.

Yes, Mother, she says simply, embracing me. I can see you are flawed. You have not hidden it. That is your greatest gift to me.

That reminds me, I say. I have a gift for you.

Oh? she says.

I have kept the little sacred figure of Nyanda—I have named her, choosing a word that floated up while I held her in my hands—carefully wrapped in my most beautiful scarf. The one of deep blue with gold stars scattered over it, like the body of Nut, goddess of Africa, and the night sky. I take it from my pocket, where I have been keeping it since I learned I would be executed, and place it in Mbati's hands.

This is for my granddaughter, I say.

Your little doll! she says, touched. You know, she says, unwrapping it, it looks like you.

No, I say, I could never have that look of confidence. Of pride. Of peace. Neither of us can have it, because self-possession will always be impossible for us to claim. But perhaps your daughter . . .

I never intended to have a child, she says. The world is entirely too treacherous. This tiny figure, she says, kissing its beaming face, against all of this. She waves her arm against the ugliness of the prison, the noise, the stench of the AIDS ward rising from below; the knowledge that I'm to be shot to death in a matter of hours.

Are you saying we should just let ourselves die out? And the hope of wholeness with us?

Oh, I don't know what I'm saying, Mother! I've stayed too long. You should rest. Good night.

Soon I shall go to bed forever, I say, shrugging. But never mind; I should get some rest. I want to be alert tomorrow, not to miss anything. *Aché Mbele,* I say.

Aché Mbele? she repeats.

Yes, I say. *Aché* is Yoruba and means "the power to make things happen." *Energy. Mbele* means "Forward!" in KiSwahili.

Oh, she says, reversing them, bowing to me: *Mbele Aché.*

She has cut my hair so that, though white, it is dense and springy, like hers. When we embrace, it is each other's hair our fingers seek.

Tashi-Evelyn-
Mrs. Johnson

Dear Lisette,

Tomorrow morning I will face the firing squad for killing someone who, many years ago, killed me. But this is no more odd, perhaps, than that I am writing this letter to you a decade after your last effort to communicate with me, and well after your own death. It is that you are in the land of death that makes friendship with you so appealing. The people of Bali, your uncle Mzee told us, think heaven is exactly like Bali. They like Bali, and so have no anxiety about dying. But if heaven is like Olinka, or even like America, there is much to be anxious about. I write to you because I will want a friend there in heaven, someone who has seriously thought about me.

I used to think my mother thought about me. But I identified with her suffering so completely it was I who always thought about, indeed was haunted by, her suffering; and because I believed she and I were one, I made the part of her that was me think about me. In truth, my mother was not equipped, there was not enough of her self left to her, to think about me. Or about my sister Dura, who bled to death after a botched circumcision, or about any of her other children. She had just sunk into her role of "She Who Prepares the Lambs for Slaughter."

Is it cruel to say this? I feel it is cruel; but that it is only the cruelty of truth, speaking it, shouting it, that will save us now. If we do not, Africa may well be depopulated of black people in our grandchildren's lifetime, and the worldwide suffering of our children will continue to be our curse.

In all my life it has been Adam and his sister, Olivia, who I believed thought most about me. He married me; she is my best friend. But do you know why my soul removed itself from Adam's reach? It is because I helped him start his progressive ministry —more progressive anyway than his father's and those of most preachers of color—in San Francisco, and I sat there in our church every Sunday for five years listening to Adam spread the word of Brotherly Love, which has its foundation in God's love of his son, Jesus Christ. I grew agitated each time he touched on the suffering of Jesus. For a long time my agitation confused me. I am a great lover of Jesus, and always have been. Still, I began to see how the constant focus on the suffering of Jesus alone excludes the suffering of others from one's view. And in my sixth year as a member of Adam's congregation, I knew I wanted my own suffering, the suffering of women and little girls, still cringing before the overpowering might and weapons of the torturers, to be the subject of a sermon. Was woman herself not the tree of life? And was she not crucified? Not in some age no one even remembers, but right now, daily, in many lands on earth?

One sermon, I begged him. One discussion with your followers about what was done to me.

He said the congregation would be embarrassed to discuss something so private and that, in any case, he would be ashamed to do so.

I'd learned to appreciate the sanctuary of the Waverly by then. A place where there was a bench on the lawn, partly in the shade but mainly in the sun, just for me. I liked my Sunday mornings there. Sedated. Calm. The grass was so green all around me, the sun so warm. The lake glittered in the distance. Out of a bag of crumbs from the kitchen, I fed the ducks.

They circumcised women, little girls, in Jesus's time. Did he know? Did the subject anger or embarrass him? Did the early church erase the record? Jesus himself was circumcised; perhaps he thought only the cutting done to him was done to women, and therefore, since he survived, it was all right.

Then there is Olivia. She has always thought so well of me. I find it impossible to disappoint her. I told her I did not kill the *tsunga* M'Lissa. I killed her all right. I placed a pillow over her face and lay across it for an hour. Her sad stories about her life caused me to lose my taste for slashing her. She had told me it was traditional for a well-appreciated *tsunga* to be murdered by someone she circumcised,

276

then burned. I carried out what was expected of me. It is curious, is it not, that the traditional tribal society dealt so cleverly with its appreciation of the *tsunga* and its hatred of her. But of course the *tsunga* was to the traditional elders merely a witch they could control, an extension of their own dominating power.

Pierre has been such a gift to me. You would be proud of him. He has promised to continue to look after Benny when I am gone. Already he has taught him more than any of his teachers ever thought he could learn. I wish you could see Pierre—and perhaps you can, through one of the windows of heaven that looks exactly like a blade of grass, or a rose, or a grain of wheat—as he continues to untangle the threads of mystery that kept me enmeshed. *Chère* Madame, he says, do you realize that the greatest curse in some African countries is not "son of a bitch" but "son of an uncircumcised mother"?

No, I do not realize it, I say.

Well, he says, it is a clue to something important! Who, for instance, were these early uncircumcised women? There is evidence that they were slaves. Slaves of other indigenous Africans and slaves of invading Arabs who swept down from the east and north. Originally bushwomen or women from the African rainforest. We know that these people, small, gentle, completely at one with their environment, liked, if you will forgive my frankness, elongated genitals. Or, put another way, they liked their genitals. So much so that they were observed from birth stroking and "pulling" on them. By the time

277

they reached puberty, well, they had acquired what was to become known, at least among European anthropologists, as "the Hottentot apron."

Enslaved among people who never touched their genitals if they could help it, having been taught such touching was a sin, these women with their generous labia and fat clitorises were considered monstrous. But what is less noted about these people, these women, is that in their own ancient societies they owned their bodies, including their vulvas, and touched them as much as they liked. In short, *Chère* Madame Johnson, early African woman, the mother of womankind, was notoriously free!

This, Lisette, is your son. I still find him absurdly small for a man, but he is big in mind. On the day of my execution, he says, he will rededicate himself to his life's work: destroying for other women—and their men—the terrors of the dark tower. A tower you told him about.

You and I will meet in heaven. I know this. Because through your son, to whom my suffering became a mystery into which he submerged himself, we have already met on earth.

Now it occurs to me to wonder how you died. If I had been able truly to understand that you would die, and cease to write to me and to exist, I would have paid better attention to you before you died. However, I was not able to comprehend death except as something that had already happened to me. Dying now does not frighten me. The execution is to take place where this government has executed so many others, the soccer field. I will refuse the blindfold so that I can see far in all directions. I will concentrate on the beauty of one blue hill in the distance, and for me, that moment will be eternity. Blessed be.

Tashi Evelyn Johnson
Reborn, soon to be Deceased

Tashi Evelyn Johnson Soul

The women along the way have been warned they must not sing. Rockjawed men with machine guns stand facing them. But women will be women. Each woman standing beside the path holds a red-beribboned, closely swaddled baby in her arms, and as I pass, the bottom wrappings fall. The women then place the babies on their shoulders or on their heads, where they kick their naked legs, smile with pleasure, screech with terror, or occasionally wave. It is a protest and celebration the men threatening them do not even recognize.

At the moment of crisis I realize that, because my hands are bound, I can not adjust my glasses, and therefore must tilt my head awkwardly in order to locate and focus on a blue hill. It is while I am distracted by this maneuver that I notice there is a blue hill rising above and just behind the women and their naked-bottomed little girls, who now stand in rows fifty feet in front of me. In front of them kneels my little band of intent faces. Mbati is unfurling a

280

banner, quickly, before the soldiers can stop her (most of them illiterate, and so their response is slow). All of them—Adam, Olivia, Benny, Pierre, Raye, Mbati—hold it firmly and stretch it wide.

RESISTANCE IS THE SECRET OF JOY! it says in huge block letters.

There is a roar as if the world cracked open and I flew inside. I am no more. And satisfied.

To the Reader

It is estimated that from ninety to one hundred million women and girls living today in African, Far Eastern and Middle Eastern countries have suffered some form of genital mutilation. Recent articles in the media have reported on the growing practice of "female circumcision" in the United States and Europe, among immigrants from countries where it is part of the culture.

Two excellent books on the subject of genital mutilation are: *Woman Why Do You Weep?*, by Asma el Dareer (London: Zed Press, 1982), and *Prisoners of Ritual: An Odyssey into Female Genital Circumcision in Africa*, by Hanny Lightfoot-Klein (Binghamton, NY: Harrington Park Press, 1989). For a look at how genital mutilation was practiced in the nineteenth-century United States, there is G. J. Barker-Benfield's book *The Horrors of the Half Known Life: Male Attitudes Toward Women and Sexuality in Nineteenth Century America* (New York: Harper & Row, 1976).

Though obviously connected, *Possessing the Secret of Joy* is not a sequel to either *The Color Purple* or *The Temple of My Familiar*. Because it is not, I have claimed the storyteller's prerogative to recast or

283

slightly change events alluded to or described in the earlier books, in order to emphasize and enhance the meanings of the present tale.

Like *The Temple of My Familiar,* it is a return to the original world of *The Color Purple* only to pick up those characters and events that refused to leave my mind. Or my spirit. Tashi, who appears briefly in *The Color Purple* and again in *The Temple of My Familiar,* stayed with me, uncommonly tenacious, through the writing of both books, and led me finally to conclude she needed, and deserved, a book of her own.

She also appeared to me in the flesh.

During the filming of *The Color Purple,* a commendable effort was made to hire Africans to act the African roles. The young woman who played Tashi, who has barely a moment on the screen, was an African from Kenya: very beautiful, graceful and poised. Seeing her brought the Tashi of my book vividly to mind, as I was reminded that in Kenya, even as this young woman was being flown to Los Angeles to act in the film, little girls were being forced under the shards of unwashed glass, tin-can tops, rusty razors and dull knives of traditional circumcisers, whom I've named *tsunga*s. Indeed, in 1982, the year *The Color Purple* was published, fourteen children died in Kenya from the effects of genital mutilation. It was only then that the president of the country banned it. It is still clandestinely practiced in Kenya, as it is still practiced, openly, in many other African countries.

Tsunga, like many of my "African" words, is made up. Perhaps it, and the other words I use, are from an

African language I used to know, now tossed up by my unconscious. I do not know from what part of Africa my African ancestors came, and so I claim the continent. I suppose I have created Olinka as my village and the Olinkans as one of my ancient, ancestral tribal peoples. Certainly I recognize Tashi as my sister.

A portion of the royalties from this book will be used to educate women and girls, men and boys, about the hazardous effects of genital mutilation, not simply on the health and happiness of individuals, but on the whole society in which it is practiced, and the world.

Mbele Aché.

Alice Walker
Costa Careyes, Mexico
Mendocino County, California
January–December, 1991

Thanks

Despite the pain one feels in honestly encountering the reality of life, I find it a wonderful time to be alive. This is because at no other time known to human beings has it been easier to give and receive energy, support and love from people never met, experiences never had.

I thank all the writers—Esther Ogunmodede, Nawal El Sadawi, Fran Hosken, Lila Said, Robin Morgan, Awa Thiam, Gloria Steinem, Fatima Abdul Mahmoud and many others around the world—for their work on the subject of genital mutilation.

I thank Monica Sjoo and Barbara Mor for the inspiration and confirmation I get from their magnificent book, *The Great Cosmic Mother: Rediscovering the Religion of the Earth.* I also thank Monica Sjoo for the beauty and psychic resonance of her visionary paintings.

I thank Carl Jung for becoming so real in my own self-therapy (by reading) that I could imagine him as alive and active in Tashi's treatment. My gift to him.

I thank my own therapist, Jane R. C., for helping me loosen some of my own knots and therefore become better able to distinguish and tackle Tashi's.

I thank Huichol culture for the amazing yarn

paintings I have admired over the past several years: paintings which flew me over the pit of so much that is static and dead in the prevailing civilization.

I thank psychologist Alice Miller for writing so strongly in defense of the child. I am especially grateful for *The Drama of the Gifted Child, Thou Shalt Not Be Aware,* and *For Your Own Good.*

I thank Louis Pascal for his unpublished essay "How AIDS Began," which introduced me to the possibility that AIDS was started by the dissemination, among Africans, of contaminated polio vaccine.

I thank the makers of the video *Born in Africa* for introducing me to the beautiful life and courageous death of Philly LuTaaya, a Ugandan musician who used his dying from AIDS to warn, educate, enlighten, inspire and love his people. This video reassured me that human compassion is equal to human cruelty and that it is up to each of us to tip the balance.

I thank Joan Miura and Mary Walsh for representing the Goddess in my household: for doing research, patching leaks, keeping the refrigerator stocked and shutting out the noise. For holding my hand as I reached for Tashi's.

I thank Robert Allen for his friendship.

I thank Jean Weisinger for her Being.

I thank my daughter Rebecca for giving me the opportunity to be a mother.